Date Due

The Presidency

KNOW YOUR GOVERNMENT

The Presidency

By Justine Rubinstein

MASON CREST
PHILADELPHIA • MIAMI

Mason Crest
450 Parkway Drive, Suite D
Broomall, Pennsylvania 19008
(866) MCP-BOOK (toll-free)
www.masoncrest.com

Printed in the United States of America
First printing
9 8 7 6 5 4 3 2 1

Series ISBN: 978-1-4222-4231-5
Hardcover ISBN: 978-1-4222-4238-4

Cataloging-in-Publication Data is available on file at the Library of Congress.

Developed and Produced by Print Matters Productions, Inc.
(www.printmattersinc.com)
Cover and Interior Design by Lori S. Malkin Design, LLC

QR CODES AND LINKS TO THIRD-PARTY CONTENT:

CONTENTS

Key Icons to Look For

Words to Understand: These words with their easy-to-understand definitions will increase readers' understanding of the text while building vocabulary skills.

Sidebars: This boxed material within the main text allows readers to build knowledge, gain insights, explore possibilities, and broaden their perspectives by weaving together additional information to provide realistic and holistic perspectives.

Educational Videos: Readers can view videos by scanning our QR codes, providing them with additional educational content to supplement the text.

Text-Dependent Questions: These questions send the reader back to the text for more careful attention to the evidence presented there.

Research Projects: Readers are pointed toward areas of further inquiry connected to each chapter. Suggestions are provided for projects that encourage deeper research and analysis.

Series Glossary of Key Terms: This back-of-the-book glossary contains terminology used throughout this series. Words found here increase the reader's ability to read and comprehend higher-level books and articles in this field.

The Evolving American Experiment

From the start, Americans have regarded their government with a mixture of reliance and mistrust. The men who founded the republic did not doubt the indispensability of government. "If men were angels," observed the 51st *Federalist Paper*, "no government would be necessary." But men are not angels. Because human beings are subject to wicked as well as to noble impulses, government was deemed essential to ensure freedom and order.

At the same time, the American revolutionaries knew that government could also become a source of injury and oppression. The men who gathered in Philadelphia in 1787 to write the Constitution therefore had two purposes in mind. They wanted to establish a strong central authority and to limit that central authority's capacity to abuse its power.

To prevent the abuse of power, the Founding Fathers wrote two basic principles into the new Constitution. The principle of federalism divided power between the state governments and the central authority. The principle of the separation of powers subdivided the central authority itself into three branches—the executive, the legislative, and the judiciary—so that "each may be a check on the other."

The Constitution did not plan the executive branch in any detail. After vesting the executive power in the president, it assumed the existence of "executive departments" without specifying what these departments should be. Congress began defining their functions in 1789 by creating the Departments of State, Treasury, and War. The secretaries in charge of these departments made up President Washington's first cabinet. Congress also provided for a legal officer, and President Washington soon invited the attorney general, as he was called, to attend cabinet meetings. As need required, Congress created more executive departments.

Setting up the cabinet was only the first step in organizing the American state. With almost no guidance from the Constitution, President Washington, seconded by Alexander Hamilton, his brilliant secretary of the treasury, equipped the infant republic with a working administrative structure. The Federalists believed in both executive energy and executive accountability and set high standards for public appointments. The Jeffersonian opposition had less faith in strong government and preferred local government to the central authority. But when Jefferson himself became president in 1801, although he set out to change the direction of policy, he found no reason to alter the framework the Federalists had erected.

By 1801, there were about 3,000 federal civilian employees in a nation of a little more than 5 million people. Growth in territory and population steadily enlarged national responsibilities. Thirty years later, when Jackson was president, there were more than 11,000 government workers in a nation of 13 million. The federal establishment was increasing at a rate faster than the population.

Jackson's presidency brought significant changes in the federal service. Jackson believed that the executive branch contained too many officials who saw their jobs as "species of property" and as "a means of promoting individual interest." Against the idea of a permanent service based on life tenure, Jackson argued for the periodic redistribution of federal offices, contending that this was the democratic way and that official duties could be made "so plain and simple that men of intelligence may readily qualify themselves for their performance." He called this policy *rotation-in-office*. His opponents called it the *spoils system*.

The United States Constitution has been the supreme law of the United States since its signing in 1787. Its first three words, "We the People," affirm that the government is here to serve the people.

In fact, partisan legend exaggerated the extent of Jackson's removals. More than 80 percent of federal officeholders retained their jobs. Jackson discharged no larger a proportion of government workers than Jefferson had done a generation earlier. But the rise in these years of mass political parties gave federal patronage new importance as a means of building the party and of rewarding activists. Jackson's successors were less restrained in the distribution of spoils. As the federal establishment grew—to nearly 40,000 by 1861—the politicization of the public service excited increasing concern.

After the Civil War, the spoils system became a major political issue. High-minded men condemned it as the root of all political evil. The spoilsmen, said the British commentator James Bryce, "have distorted and depraved the mechanism of politics." Patronage—giving jobs to unqualified, incompetent, and dishonest persons—lowered the standards of public service and nourished corrupt political machines. Office-seekers pursued presidents and cabinet secretaries without mercy. "Patronage," said Ulysses S. Grant after his presidency, "is the bane of the presidential office." "Every time I appoint someone to office," said another political leader, "I make a hundred enemies and one ingrate." George William Curtis, the president of the National Civil Service Reform League, summed up the indictment:

> The theory which perverts public trusts into party spoils, making public employment dependent upon personal favor and not on proved merit, necessarily ruins the self-respect of public employees, destroys the function of party in a republic, prostitutes elections into a desperate strife for personal profit, and degrades the national character by lowering the moral tone and standard of the country.

The object of civil service reform was to promote efficiency and honesty in the public service and to bring about the ethical regeneration of public life. In 1883, over bitter opposition from politicians, the reformers passed the Pendleton Act, establishing a bipartisan Civil Service Commission, competitive examinations, and appointment on merit. The Pendleton Act also gave the president authority to extend by executive order the number of "classified" jobs—that is, jobs subject to the merit system. The act applied initially only to about 14,000 of the more than 100,000 federal positions. But by the end of the nineteenth century, 40 percent of federal jobs had moved into the classified category.

The twentieth century saw a considerable expansion of the federal establishment. The Great Depression and the New Deal led the national government to take on a variety of new responsibilities. The New Deal extended the federal regulatory apparatus. By 1940, in a nation of 130 million people, the number of federal workers for the first time passed the 1 million mark. The Second World War brought federal civilian employment to 3.8 million in 1945. With peace, the federal establishment declined to around 2 million by 1950. Then growth resumed, reaching 2.8 million by the 1980s. In 2017, there were only 2.1 million federal civilian employees.

The New Deal years saw rising criticism of "big government" and "bureaucracy." Businessmen resented federal regulation. Conservatives worried about the impact of paternalistic government on individual self-reliance, on community responsibility, and on economic and personal freedom. The nation, in effect, renewed the old debate between Hamilton and Jefferson in the early republic.

Since the 1980s, with the presidency of Ronald Reagan, this debate has burst out with unusual intensity. According to conservatives, government intervention abridges liberty, stifles enterprise, and is inefficient, wasteful, and arbitrary. It disturbs the harmony of the self-adjusting market and creates worse troubles than it solves. "Get government off our backs," according to the popular cliché, and our problems will solve themselves. When government is necessary, let it be at the local level, close to the people.

In fact, for all the talk about the "swollen" and "bloated" bureaucracy, the federal establishment has not been growing as inexorably as many Americans seem to believe. In 1949, it consisted of 2.1 million people. Nearly 70 years later, while the country had grown by 177 million, the federal force is the same. Federal workers were a smaller percentage of the population in 2017 than they were in 1985, 1955, or 1940. The federal establishment, in short, has not kept pace with population growth. Moreover, national defense and security-related agencies account for nearly 70 percent of federal employment.

Why, then, the widespread idea about the remorseless growth of government? It is partly because in the 1960s, the national government assumed new and intrusive functions: affirmative action in civil rights, environmental protection, safety and health in the workplace, community organization, legal aid to the poor. Although this enlargement of the federal regulatory role was accompanied by marked growth in the size of government on all levels, the expansion has taken place primarily in state and local government. Whereas the federal force increased by only 27 percent in the 30 years after 1950, the state and local government forces increased by an astonishing 212 percent.

In general, Americans do not want less government. What they want is *more efficient* government. For a time in the 1970s, with the Vietnam War and Watergate, Americans lost confidence in the national government. In 1964, more than three-quarters of those polled had thought the national government could be trusted to do right most of the time. By 1980, only one-quarter was prepared to offer such trust. After reaching a three-decade high in the wake of the 9/11 terrorist attacks, public confidence in the federal government was near historic lows in 2017 at just 18 percent.

Two hundred years after the drafting of the Constitution, Americans still regard government with a mixture of reliance and mistrust—a good combination. Mistrust is the best way to keep government reliable. Informed criticism is the means of correcting governmental inefficiency, incompetence, and arbitrariness; that is, of best enabling government to play its essential role. For without government, we cannot attain the goals of the Founding Fathers. Without an understanding of government, we cannot have the informed criticism that makes government do the job right. It is the duty of every American citizen to know our government—which is what this series is all about.

Inauguration

Every American president begins his term in office with the same sentence: "I do solemnly swear (or affirm) that I will faithfully execute the office of President of the United States, and will to the best of my ability, preserve, protect, and defend the Constitution of the United States."

Since April 30, 1789, when George Washington stepped onto the balcony of Federal Hall in New York City, 44 men have begun their terms as president with the same phrase. But all of these men have put their own stamp on the office of president of the United States, and the executive branch has evolved as a reflection of their personalities and their visions for the country.

Today, when we think about our national government, the president is often the clearest and most visible symbol of that government at work. But when the Founding Fathers first met in Philadelphia in 1787 to discuss how to shape the new government that would become the United States, the scope

In 1789, George Washington took the oath as the first president of the United States. His eight-page inaugural address was handwritten and read aloud on the steps of Federal Hall in New York City. His speech has been preserved and can be found at the National Archives.

Fellow Citizens of the Senate
and
of the House of Representatives.

Among the vicissitudes
incident to life, no event could have
filled me with greater anxieties than
that of which the notification was
transmitted by your order, and received on the fourteenth day of the
present month: ____ On the one hand,
I was summoned by my Country, whose
voice I can never hear but with venera-
tion and love, from a retreat which
I had chosen with the fondest predi-
lection, and, in my flattering hopes,
with an immutable decision, as the
asylum of my declining years: a retreat which was rendered every day
more necessary as well as more dear
to me, by the addition of habit to in-
clination, and of frequent interrup-
tions in my health to the gradual waste
committed on it by time. ____ On the
other hand, the magnitude and dif-
ficulty of the trust to which the voice
of my Country called me, being suffici-
ent to awaken in the wisest and most
experienced of her citizens, a distrust
ful

This 1889 painting by Ramon de Elorriaga, The Inauguration of George Washington, *depicts his swearing-in on April 30, 1789, at Federal Hall in New York City.*

of the presidency sparked intense debate. Some questioned the need for a single individual to lead the government, fearing that a strong head of government would quickly lead to a **monarchy**. It soon became clear, however, that the leader of the new government must have enough power to be independent of the legislature and to ensure that the federal government would not be at the mercy of the state governments.

Other debates centered on how the new executive would be elected—by popular vote, by designated electors, or by Congress—and how long his or her term in office would last. Another debate focused on whether the chief executive should have a specified council of advisors, perhaps from specific branches of the government, such as the president of the Senate and the chief justice of the Supreme Court, or from specific areas of the country, like a representative from the East, the Middle States, and the South.

When it became clear that George Washington, hero of the Revolutionary War, would be the first nominee for president of the United States, many of the debates were resolved. The idea of a council of advisors was set aside; the Constitution does not even call for a "cabinet." The president was given the right of veto power over legislation. He was given the right to appoint people to office "in all not otherwise provided for." He was given the title of "Commander in Chief."

The final results of the debates and discussions outlined the terms, seen in Article II of the U.S. Constitution, that govern the presidency—terms that have, with only a few additional amendments, dictated the scope of the office for more than 200 years. The Constitution notes that the president shall hold office for four years. It states how the president shall be elected and removed from office.

The Constitution specifies that the president must be a natural-born citizen of the United States (a citizen who was born in this country). The president must be at least 35 years old and have lived within the United States for at least 14 years.

The Constitution notes that the president should be paid for the service performed and that the salary should neither increase nor decrease during the president's term in office. It notes the oath of office that must be spoken for each new president.

The Constitution also states that the president has the power to grant **reprieves** and **pardons**, to make treaties, and to appoint ambassadors and judges of the Supreme Court. Finally, the Constitution states that the president should periodically give Congress information on the state of the Union, and be responsible for executing the laws of the United States faithfully.

These broad but simple guidelines provided an outline of the office of the president for the first man to hold that title. It was up to future presidents to fill in the details that would make the office of president one of the most powerful in the world.

The First President

Just as the drafters of the Constitution had George Washington in mind when considering the position of president, Washington himself, as the first holder of the office, placed an imprint on the presidency that would last more than two centuries. Washington understood that he was setting precedents that future presidents would follow, and it is to his credit that so many of the standards he set would prove to be valuable guidelines for the nation's leadership.

Washington created a strong cabinet of four men, including Thomas Jefferson as secretary of state and Alexander Hamilton as secretary of the treasury. All loans and debts that the country undertook were subject to Washington's approval. Washington also required his approval for any use of the seal of the United States. He successfully used his popularity to build a strong relationship with Congress, and he was careful to treat members of the Senate and the House of Representatives with respect. He felt strongly that the presidency must be dignified, using symbols and ceremony when necessary. He set the precedent of serving only two terms as president, and all future presidents (with one exception—Franklin D. Roosevelt, who was elected to four terms in office) would follow this example. In fact, Washington had wanted to serve only one term but reluctantly agreed to serve an additional four years. He was so popular that it seems certain he could have been elected president for life had he so chosen. The Twenty-Second Amendment to the Constitution (ratified in 1951) limited future presidents to two terms.

Washington set an example that other presidents would follow of traveling around the country so that people throughout the United States could have an opportunity to see their leader and so that he would be familiar with various states and their differing needs. Washington assumed that the president would be actively involved in shaping foreign and domestic policy, and his assertive attitude toward both ensured that future presidents would clearly be at the head of government policymaking.

After his inauguration, George Washington stepped out on to the balcony to greet the people of the United States.

In the Beginning

Just as every presidency begins with the same oath of office, so every presidency begins with a ceremony known as the **inauguration**. It marks the transition from one president to the next; it is the official beginning of a new administration. With the recitation of the oath of office, a private citizen formally becomes president. The results of a presidential election are decided weeks earlier, with the tallying of electoral votes, but it is the inauguration that formally marks the time when a president begins his term in office.

Again, this precedent was set by George Washington, who traveled from his home in Mount Vernon, Virginia, to the nation's capital (then located in New York City) after being informed of his election on April 14, 1789. Ceremonies, parades, and the sound of ringing bells and booming cannons accompanied him on his trip north. Parties and celebrations in New York delayed the official inauguration

An 1845 lithograph by Nathaniel Currier shows George Washington being greeted by a group of women in Trenton, NJ, as he travels to his inauguration in New York City. Ceremonies and parades followed Washington as he made his way from his home in Virginia to New York.

for several days. During the time before the inauguration, one final debate raged: Exactly what would the leader of the new nation be called? Among the proposals was "His Highness the President of the United States of America and Protector of Their Liberties." In the end, it was decided that the chief executive would be simply known as "The President of the United States."

The first inauguration drew large crowds to New York. Washington began the tradition of delivering an inaugural address (or speech) at the ceremony. In his first address, Washington expressed his conflicted feelings about accepting the call to serve as president. Washington also noted his decision to refuse any payment for his service as president. This was one of the few acts Washington took that did not become a precedent for future presidents.

Many notable events have marked presidential inaugurations over the years. Washington began the custom of taking the oath of office outdoors, and he used the phrase "So help me God" after the oath. There was an inaugural ball after Washington's inauguration, but because of other business, it was not held until May 7. First Lady Martha Washington did not travel to New York for her husband's inauguration.

In his second inauguration, on March 4, 1793, Washington set a record of sorts. He delivered the shortest inaugural address—a mere 135 words.

John Adams, the second president, began the custom of receiving the oath from the chief justice of the Supreme Court. Thomas Jefferson, the third president, was the first to take the oath of office in the new capital, Washington, D.C.

Martin Van Buren (1837) started the custom of having the outgoing (Andrew Jackson) and incoming presidents ride together to the Capitol for the inauguration. African Americans first participated in the inaugural parade in 1865, when Abraham Lincoln began his second term in office. Women did not participate in an inaugural parade until 1917, when Woodrow Wilson began his second term as president.

The Twentieth Amendment to the Constitution changed the inaugural date to January 20, specifying that the president's term would end at noon on that date. Franklin D. Roosevelt was the first president to be inaugurated on that date, beginning his second term as president on January 20, 1937.

Watch footage from a presidential inauguration.

WASHINGTON'S SECOND INAUGURAL ADDRESS

On March 4, 1793, George Washington delivered his second inaugural address in the city that was then serving as the nation's capital, Philadelphia. Like so many of Washington's acts, this one was noteworthy—as the shortest inaugural speech given by any president.

Fellow Citizens:

I am again called upon by the voice of my country to execute the functions of its Chief Magistrate. When the occasion proper for it shall arrive, I shall endeavor to express the high sense I entertain of this distinguished honor, and of the confidence which has been reposed in me by the people of united America.

Previous to the execution of any official act of the President the Constitution requires an oath of office. This oath I am now about to take, and in your presence: That if it shall be found during my administration of the Government I have in any instance violated willingly or knowingly the injunctions thereof, I may (besides incurring constitutional punishment) be subject to the upbraidings of all who are now witnesses of the present solemn ceremony.

The first inauguration to be televised was in 1949, when Harry Truman began his second term in office. And it was Bill Clinton's second inauguration, in 1997, that marked the first live broadcast of the ceremony on the Internet.

Inaugurations Today

Inaugurations for modern presidents follow many of the precedents set long ago. Presidents-elect have attended a morning worship service before the inaugural ceremony since 1933. The outgoing president then accompanies the president-elect to the swearing-in ceremony at the Capitol.

The chief justice of the Supreme Court administers the oath of office. After the swearing-in, the new president delivers an inaugural address, which generally outlines his plans for his term in office. George Washington's second inaugural address was the shortest; the longest, delivered by William Henry Harrison in 1841, was 8,445 words—so long that Harrison began the address, stopped to take the oath of office, and then resumed the speech. Harrison died one month later of pneumonia, believed to have been caused by prolonged exposure to bitterly cold weather on his Inauguration Day.

Some presidents have used the inaugural address to deliver inspiring messages to the nation that have lasted long after their terms ended. In 1865, as the Civil War was drawing to an end, Abraham Lincoln encouraged the nation: "With malice toward none, with charity for all, with firmness in the right as God gives us to see the right, let us strive on to finish the work we are in, to bind up the nation's wounds, to care for him who shall have borne the battle and for his widow and his orphan, to do all which may achieve and cherish a just and lasting peace among ourselves and with all nations." In 1933, as the Great Depression swept over the United States, Franklin D. Roosevelt's inaugural address contained the bracing message: "The only thing we have to fear is fear itself." And in 1961, John F. Kennedy encouraged a new generation to "ask not what your country can do for you—ask what you can do for your country."

After the inaugural ceremony, the new president, vice president, and guests enjoy a luncheon at the U.S. Capitol. The president views an inaugural parade from

Four presidents—past, present, and future—attended the inauguration of John F. Kennedy in January 1961. During his transition, Kennedy spent time with his predecessor, Dwight Eisenhower.

a viewing stand, and later a series of inaugural balls are held in the president's honor. The number has varied over the years—in 1997, 14 such balls in Washington, D.C., marked President Bill Clinton's inauguration.

For more than two centuries, a president's term in office has begun in the same way—with an inauguration and with the same oath of office. But within that simple vow to "preserve, protect, and defend the Constitution of the United States," an extraordinary range of power and responsibility is placed on each new president. What exactly does it mean to be the president of the United States? How does the president shape policy? How has the president's role changed over the years? In the chapters that follow, we will discover the answers to these questions and learn what it is like to be the president of the United States.

Text-Dependent Questions

1. How many years must someone have lived within the United States in order to hold the office of president?

2. Who was the first president to take the inaugural oath in the nation's capital of Washington, D.C.?

3. What president gave the longest inaugural address?

Research Project

Research an inaugural address from presidential history. It could be from any president or era, and either a first or second (or, in the case of Franklin Roosevelt, third or fourth) inaugural address. Read the text carefully, and write an analysis of its key points, what the president was intending to communicate, and the historical events that inspired his words. Include information about the public's reaction to the speech, if available, as well as perspectives of historians or biographers.

The President and the Constitution

The rules that shape the presidency, stating who can be president, what the president's powers will be, and how long he or she will serve, are found in the Constitution. In several paragraphs, the presidency is defined.

These paragraphs, though, were among the most difficult to resolve when the men charged with creating the Constitution met in Philadelphia in 1787. The debates over the presidency were among the bitterest disagreements at the Constitutional Convention.

The 55 delegates to the convention represented 12 of the 13 original states. (Rhode Island did not send delegates.) For the most part, they agreed about the need to shape a new system of government. They largely agreed that the government should be divided into separate branches—the executive, judicial, and legislative branches—to ensure a balance of power.

The Founding Fathers—Benjamin Franklin, John Adams, George Washington, Thomas Paine, and Thomas Jefferson.

George Washington is shown in this 1856 painting by Junius Brutus Stearns, George Washington Addressing the Constitutional Convention. *One issue debated at the Constitutional Convention in 1787 was whether the executive branch would consist of several men acting as a council or would be led by a single individual. Other issues involved veto powers and the term of office.*

But the question of what the executive branch would involve exposed the fears and misgivings of the delegates.

The initial proposal was that the executive branch would consist of several men, forming a kind of committee or council. The issues that had led to the Revolutionary War were still fresh in the minds of the delegates, and many feared duplicating the same form of government—a monarchy ruled by a king—that they had so recently fought against.

James Wilson, from Pennsylvania, was the one who first proposed the idea of an executive branch headed by a single individual. A long silence followed

THE PRESIDENCY

his suggestion, finally broken by Edmund Randolph of Virginia, who reminded Wilson that a single executive might be the beginning of a monarchy in the United States.

Another proposal, from Roger Sherman of Connecticut, focused on how the members of the executive branch would be chosen. Sherman felt that the executive branch's responsibility should be to carry out the will of the American people, as expressed by the legislative branch. In Sherman's proposal, the executive branch would report to the legislative branch, and the legislative branch would decide what business the executive branch should handle and how many executives should be appointed at any one time.

Some—but not all—of the objections became more muted as it became clear that George Washington, who was serving as the president of the Constitutional

Roger Sherman, a delegate to the Constitutional Convention from Connecticut, thought that the executive branch should report to the legislative branch. He also was opposed to the idea of allowing the person leading the executive branch to be re-elected.

Convention, might become the first "chief executive." The scope of the powers of this "president," as the chief executive became known, also drew concern. Some feared the idea of a president powerful enough to serve as commander in chief and also make treaties and appoint government officials. Others worried about how the president would be chosen, fearing that few men would be popular enough to win a clear majority of the votes. Still others worried about what would happen if the president were to prove unwilling to give up his office, warning of the dangers of a president "for life."

This question of how long a president should serve was a critical one for many of the delegates. Wilson, the delegate who initially proposed a single executive, or president, favored a three-year term, with the idea that after this short period a president might be eligible for re-election. Sherman and others opposed the idea of re-election, believing that a single term provided the best protection for the country against a president who might prove unworthy once in office. Still others favored a single term of seven years, or a fixed number of terms after which a president could no longer be elected.

It took four months for the delegates to resolve their disagreements and emerge from Philadelphia with a Constitution for the United States. The debates did not end with the final Constitution, however. Many continued to question the need for a president and expressed their concerns about limiting his powers. The questions about who should be president, and how much power should be connected to the office, continue to this day.

The Rough Draft

The earliest draft of the document that would eventually become the Constitution was known as "the Virginia Plan" and was presented to the Constitutional Convention by the governor of Virginia, Edmund Randolph. Most experts agree that its author was probably James Madison.

The Virginia Plan called for a "National Executive," to be chosen by the "National Legislature" (or Congress). The number of years this executive would serve was left blank, but a note was included that said the executive could not serve more than one term.

It is interesting to look at the Virginia Plan and the earliest debates at the convention to see how the United States might have become quite a different nation had the delegates not revised their plans for the presidency. The initial agreement among the delegates was that the president would serve one term of seven years and that he could not be re-elected after those seven years.

The proposal to have the executive chosen by Congress proved unworkable. It destroyed the idea of balance of power by giving too much influence to the legislative branch. The delegates decided to combine the proposals of a president chosen by popular vote and by representatives of the people with an "**Electoral College**." States would be divided into a certain number of districts (in the rough draft this number was left blank), and voters would elect a certain number of representatives (again, the number was left blank), who would meet and elect by ballot the person who would become the chief executive. It was noted that the Electoral College could not select one of its own members to serve as chief executive.

Learn more about the Electoral College.

Later discussions determined that the state legislatures should choose the "electors" who would make up the Electoral College. The question of how long the president should serve arose again. Another proposal at this early stage was that the president should serve for six years and be eligible for re-election, but also that he or she could be **impeached** if he or she should prove incompetent.

The Virginia Plan also called for the executive branch to have a "veto power" (a power to reject acts of the legislature), and this was also hammered out in the debates. Benjamin Franklin argued against the chief executive being able to veto acts of Congress, having seen this power abused by the governor of his state of Pennsylvania.

Next, the delegates debated the question of what power the president should have to appoint other officials. The delegates decided that the president could have the power to pick federal judges but that the Senate would have the power to reject any nominees if a majority of its members agreed.

The first draft of the Constitution described a president (using the term "president" instead of "chief executive" or "executive") appointed by the Congress who would serve a single seven-year term. The president would have the power to veto acts of Congress, would command the armed forces, and could be impeached and removed from office.

Continuing Debates

Once this rough draft was circulated, the debates about the presidency began again. The delegates agreed that the president must meet certain standards—he or she must be a certain age and must have been a citizen of the United States for a specific period of time. There was disagreement, though, about what other qualifications the president should have.

One delegate—Charles Pinckney of South Carolina—felt that the people selected to serve in the executive, legislative, and judicial branches of the government should all be required to own a certain amount of property, suggesting that wealth would keep them independent. Pinckney's idea was that the president's personal wealth should be at least $100,000, a considerable sum in those days. This point was hotly debated by several delegates, including Benjamin Franklin, who argued that the United States should not demonstrate such clear **favoritism** for the wealthy.

Other debates focused on whether the Congress or the president should have war powers. It was decided that the president should have the ability to respond in the event of a sudden attack, although the Constitution gives Congress the power to declare war.

There was discussion about whether a council of advisors to the president, or a "cabinet," should be included in the Constitution. Debate focused on who these members might be—one proposal was for the cabinet to consist of the president of the Senate, the chief justice of the Supreme Court, and the ministers of foreign and domestic affairs, war, and finance.

There was also debate about who should replace the president if he or she were to die, resign, or be forced from office. Proposals stated that the duties of the president would be performed by the president of the Senate, the chief justice, the members of the cabinet, or a suitable candidate chosen by Congress should the need arise.

With all of the competing proposals and debates, it is astonishing that the majority of the delegates finally signed the polished and revised Constitution on September 17, 1787. The required nine states ratified the document by June 21, 1788. The questions of who would serve as president, for how long, and what powers he or she would have, were resolved—as least for a while.

Benjamin Franklin (left) addressed the Constitutional Convention. Franklin spoke against a proposal by Charles Pinckney (right) of South Carolina that would have required the president to have a personal wealth of at least $100,000, a princely sum in those days. Franklin did not want such favoritism to be shown to the wealthy.

In the Constitution

Several portions of the Constitution pertain to the presidency. It is interesting to compare what was discussed in the debates with what became the final text of the Constitution.

Article 1, Section 7

. . . Every bill which shall have passed the House of Representatives and the Senate shall, before it become a law, be presented to the President of the United States; if he approve he shall sign it, but if not he shall return it, with his objections to that House in which it shall have originated, who shall enter the objections at large on their Journal, and proceed to reconsider it. If after such reconsideration two thirds of

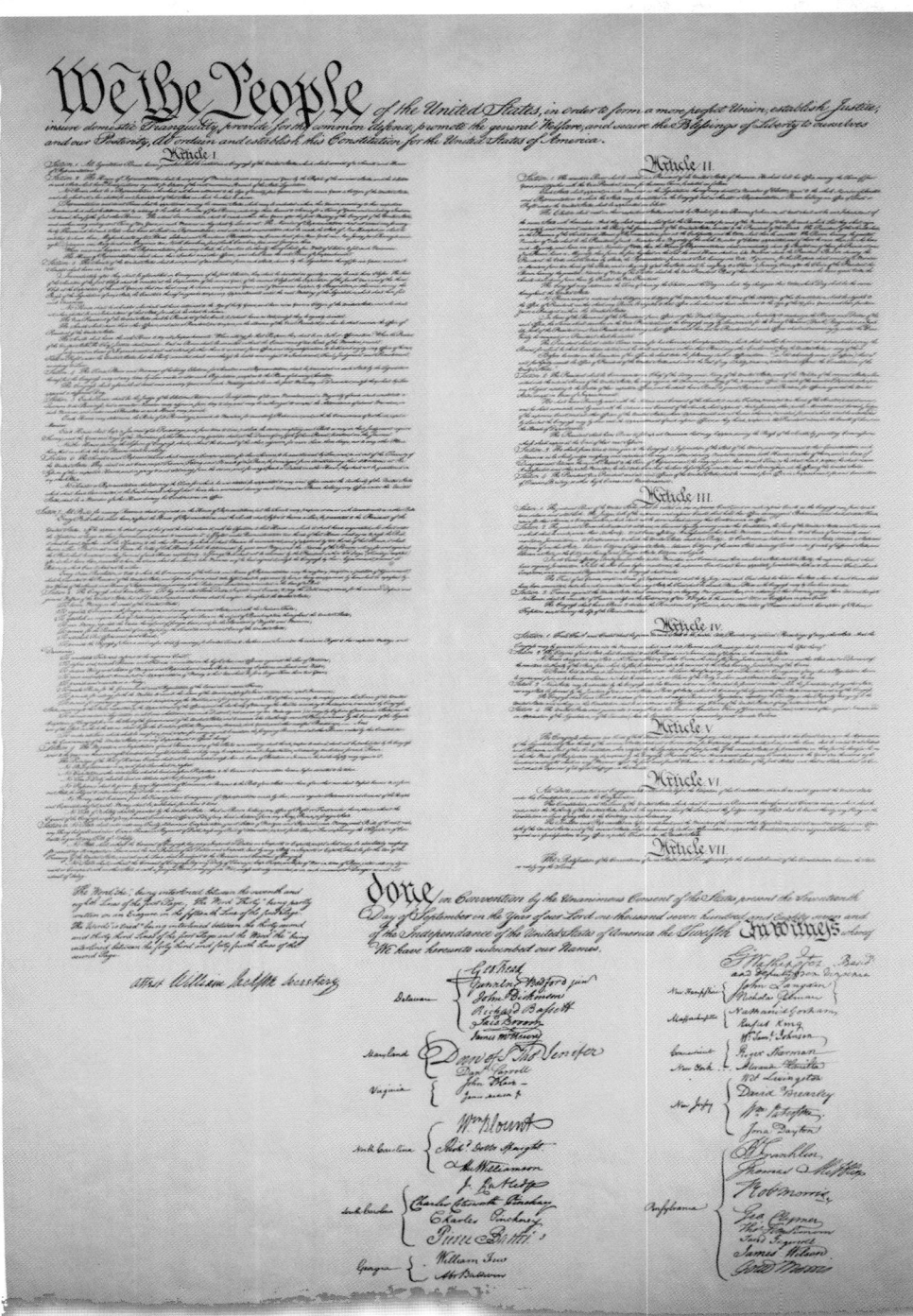

that House shall agree to pass the bill, it shall be sent, together with the objections, to the other House, by which it shall likewise be reconsidered, and if approved by two thirds of that House, it shall become a law. . . .

Article II, Section 1

The executive power shall be vested in a President of the United States of America. He shall hold his office during the term of four years, and, together with the Vice President, chosen for the same term, be elected, as follows.

Each state shall appoint, in such manner as the Legislature thereof may direct, a number of electors, equal to the whole number of senators and representatives to which the state may be entitled in the Congress: but no senator or representative, or person holding an office of trust or profit under the United States, shall be appointed an elector. . . .

No person except a natural born citizen, or a citizen of the United States, at the time of the adoption of this Constitution, shall be eligible to the office of president; neither shall any person be eligible to that office who shall not have attained to the age of thirty five years, and been fourteen years a resident within the United States.

In case of the removal of the President from office, or of his death, resignation, or inability to discharge the powers and duties of the said office, the same shall devolve on the Vice President, and the Congress may by law provide for the case of removal, death, resignation or inability, both of the President and Vice President, declaring what officer shall then act as President, and such officer shall act accordingly, until the disability be removed, or a President shall be elected.

The President shall, at stated times, receive for his services, a compensation, which shall neither be increased nor diminished during the period for which he shall have been elected. . . .

Before he enter on the execution of his office, he shall take the following oath or affirmation:—"I do solemnly swear (or affirm) that I will faithfully execute the office of President of the United States, and will to the best of my ability, preserve, protect and defend the Constitution of the United States."

Article II, Section 2

The President shall be Commander in Chief of the Army and Navy of the United States, and of the militia of the several states. . . .

He shall have power, by and with the advice and consent of the Senate, to make treaties, provided two thirds of the senators present concur; and he shall nominate, and by and with the advice and consent of the Senate, shall appoint ambassadors, other public ministers and consuls, judges of the Supreme Court, and all other officers of the United States, whose appointments are not herein otherwise provided for. . . .

Article II, Section 3

He shall from time to time give to the Congress information of the State of the Union, and recommend to their consideration such measures as he shall judge necessary and expedient. . . . He shall take care that the laws be faithfully executed, and shall commission all the officers of the United States.

Article II, Section 4

The President, Vice President and all civil officers of the United States, shall be removed from office on impeachment for, and conviction of, treason, bribery, or other high crimes and misdemeanors.

Amendments

The Constitution, particularly Article II, provided the initial definition of the presidency. Later amendments to the Constitution would offer additional clarification to the office.

The Twelfth Amendment, ratified in 1804, added further details about the Electoral College, and how the president and vice president would be elected. Until that time, the presidential candidate receiving the greatest number of votes would become president; the runner-up would become vice president. This created an unworkable situation in which representatives from different political parties, often with vastly different visions for the country, would then be expected to join together cooperatively as president and vice president. In the Twelfth Amendment, candidates would then clearly run for election as either president or vice president.

The beginning of the presidential term was changed from March 4 to January 20 (a new term beginning at noon on that day) in the Twentieth Amendment, ratified in 1933. In 1951, the Twenty-Second Amendment specified that the president

	President	Term in office
1.	George Washington	April 30, 1789–March 4, 1797
2.	John Adams	March 4, 1797–March 4, 1801
3.	Thomas Jefferson	March 4, 1801–March 4, 1809
4.	James Madison	March 4, 1809–March 4, 1817
5.	James Monroe	March 4, 1817–March 4, 1825
6.	John Quincy Adams	March 4, 1825–March 4, 1829
7.	Andrew Jackson	March 4, 1829–March 4, 1837
8.	Martin Van Buren	March 4, 1837–March 4, 1841
9.	William Henry Harrison	March 4, 1841–April 4, 1841
10.	John Tyler	April 4, 1841–March 4, 1845
11.	James Polk	March 4, 1845–March 4, 1849
12.	Zachary Taylor	March 4, 1849–July 9, 1850
13.	Millard Fillmore	July 9, 1850–March 4, 1853
14.	Franklin Pierce	March 4, 1853–March 4, 1857
15.	James Buchanan	March 4, 1857–March 4, 1861
16.	Abraham Lincoln	March 4, 1861–April 15, 1865
17.	Andrew Johnson	April 15, 1865–March 4, 1869
18.	Ulysses Grant	March 4, 1869–March 4, 1877
19.	Rutherford Hayes	March 4, 1877–March 4, 1881
20.	James Garfield	March 4, 1881–September 19, 1881
21.	Chester Arthur	September 19, 1881–March 4, 1885
22.	Grover Cleveland	March 4, 1885–March 4, 1889
23.	Benjamin Harrison	March 4, 1889–March 4, 1893
24.	Grover Cleveland	March 4, 1893–March 4, 1897

(continued on page 32)

(continued from page 31)

25.	William McKinley	March 4, 1897–September 14, 1901
26.	Theodore Roosevelt	September 14, 1901–March 4, 1909
27.	William Taft	March 4, 1909–March 4, 1913
28.	Woodrow Wilson	March 4, 1913–March 4, 1921
29.	Warren Harding	March 4, 1921–August 2, 1923
30.	Calvin Coolidge	August 2, 1923–March 4, 1929
31.	Herbert Hoover	March 4, 1929–March 4, 1933
32.	Franklin Roosevelt	March 4, 1933–April 12, 1945
33.	Harry Truman	April 12, 1945–January 20, 1953
34.	Dwight Eisenhower	January 20, 1953–January 20, 1961
35.	John Kennedy	January 20, 1961–November 22, 1963
36.	Lyndon Johnson	November 22, 1963–January 20, 1969
37.	Richard Nixon	January 20, 1969–August 9, 1974
38.	Gerald Ford	August 9, 1974–January 20, 1977
39.	Jimmy Carter	January 20, 1977–January 20, 1981
40.	Ronald Reagan	January 20, 1981–January 20, 1989
41.	George H.W. Bush	January 20, 1989–January 20, 1993
42.	William J. Clinton	January 20, 1993–January 20, 2001
43.	George W. Bush	January 20, 2001–January 20, 2009
44.	Barack Obama	January 20, 2009–January 20, 2017
45.	Donald Trump	January 20, 2017–

would be limited to two terms. (President Franklin D. Roosevelt had been elected to four terms as president but died before completing his fourth term.) The Twenty-Fifth Amendment, ratified in 1967, gave the president the power, with approval from Congress, to appoint a vice president when the vice presidency became vacant. (President Richard Nixon soon had to follow this amendment, appointing Gerald Ford to the vice presidency in 1973 when Vice President Spiro Agnew was forced to resign.) The Twenty-Fifth Amendment also specified that the vice president would become president if the president were to die, resign, or be removed from office. Once again, this amendment would apply to Gerald Ford, who became president when Richard Nixon resigned in 1974.

Other amendments to the Constitution—those amendments that specify who has the right to vote—have shaped the presidency. The Fifteenth Amendment, ratified in 1870, gave the right to vote to black people. Women were given the right to vote in 1920, with the ratification of the Nineteenth Amendment. And eighteen-year-olds gained the right to vote in 1971 with passage of the Twenty-Sixth Amendment. (Previously, voters needed to be at least 21 years of age).

Text-Dependent Questions

1. Which state did not send delegates to the Constitutional Convention in 1787?

2. What is meant by "veto power?"

3. What does the Twelfth Amendment specify?

Research Project

Research the Electoral College, including its history, the number of electors and how votes are distributed among states, and ways that the College impacts presidential campaigns and elections. Write a brief report summarizing your findings.

Bonus: Include a section analyzing arguments for and against the Electoral College. How does each side frame the role of the Electoral College, the popular vote, the rise of "swing states" and their effect on voter turnout, and other related issues?

The Powers of the President

Words to Understand

Acquit: To clear a person of a charge or offense.

Diplomat: An official representative of one country to another.

Patronage: When an official gives appointments or favors to supporters and friends.

Repeal: To formally declare a law or government act no longer valid.

Resolution: A formal proposal adopted by a governing body.

The Constitution spelled out several powers reserved for the executive branch. These included the power to serve as commander in chief of the armed forces, the power to make treaties, the power to make political appointments, and the power to veto certain acts of Congress. Throughout history, presidents have chosen to exercise these powers in different ways. Sometimes they have tested the limits of the Constitution or proved the wisdom of the Founding Fathers in granting these powers to the presidency.

The Constitution gives the president the power to serve as "Commander in Chief of the Army and Navy of the United States, and of the Militia of the several States." The U.S. military has expanded well beyond

This painting depicts Andrew Jackson at the Battle of New Orleans.

the small volunteer forces initially envisioned by the delegates to the Constitutional Convention, and the power to serve as commander in chief places in the president's hands access to a large, well-equipped fighting force and a wide array of weapons systems, including nuclear weapons.

What happens when presidents choose to exercise this power? And how many presidents have the kind of military experience necessary to truly direct the armed forces of the United States?

George Washington's experience as a Revolutionary War hero made him the clear choice to be the country's first president, and his proven skills in battle made it seem apparent that a president could serve as commander in chief. In fact, Washington actually did lead soldiers in the field after becoming president, riding at the head of troops to put down a rebellious force of some 6,000 men who had assembled near Pittsburgh to protest a tax on whiskey. It would be the first and only time a sitting president would lead troops into the field.

As president, James Madison was present at Bladensburg, Maryland, when American forces were defeated by British troops and forced to retreat during the War of 1812. The British then marched to Washington, burning government buildings, including the Capitol and the White House. President Abraham Lincoln traveled to Fort Stevens in Washington, D.C., in July 1864 to survey the scene when his Union soldiers came under fire from Confederate forces. Lincoln was quickly rushed back to the White House.

In more recent years, presidents have traveled to war zones to meet with U.S. forces, but safety and security concerns make it impossible to imagine contemporary presidents leading troops into conflict. Presidents have sent Americans into combat both close to and far from U.S. soil.

Washington was the first, but certainly not the last, president to be elected based on a successful military career. Andrew Jackson became a military hero after his success at the Battle of New Orleans during the War of 1812. Jackson had also served in the Continental Army during the Revolutionary War and is the only American president to have been held as a prisoner of war. William Henry Harrison also had a distinguished military career during the War of 1812, earning fame for his command of troops during the Battle of the Thames. Zachary Taylor's military achievements during the Mexican-American War made him a national hero and, later, a successful candidate for president. Ulysses Grant earned fame as a commander of Union troops during the Civil War. Theodore Roosevelt's achievements during the Spanish-American War brought him national attention, and Dwight Eisenhower was sought after as a presidential candidate by both the Republican and Democratic parties after his service as supreme allied commander during World War II.

Although military service is not a requirement for the presidency, many of the men who have become president have had some form of military service. Not all, however, have seen active combat. In fact, only a few former presidents have not served in the military, militia, or reserves. These include John Adams, Thomas Jefferson, John Quincy Adams, Martin Van Buren, Millard Fillmore, Grover Cleveland, William Howard Taft, Woodrow Wilson, Warren Harding, Calvin Coolidge, Herbert Hoover, Franklin D. Roosevelt, Bill Clinton, Barack Obama, and Donald Trump.

Theodore Roosevelt leads the Rough Riders into battle during the Spanish-American War. Several presidents parlayed their success on the battlefield into a run for the nation's highest office.

Making War

Although the president serves as commander in chief, the Constitution does not give him or her the power to declare war. This power lies with Congress. The president, however, does have the power to respond if the nation is suddenly attacked, in instances where speed and secrecy might matter.

This has created a number of problems throughout American history. The most obvious is the question of defining what a war is. Presidents have sent American troops into conflict without a congressional declaration of war. Congress has only declared war in five conflicts—the War of 1812, the Mexican-American War, the Spanish-American War, World War I, and World War II. There are other instances where presidents have sought congressional authorization for the use of military forces; these have included the Vietnam War, the Persian Gulf War, the invasion of Afghanistan following the September 11, 2001, attacks on U.S. soil, and the war in Iraq that began in 2003.

Presidents do have the power to order the military to stop fighting or to withdraw from a region in conflict. They have the power to negotiate treaties with an enemy power. If Congress issues an official declaration of war, however, then it must also take some official action to end the state of war between the United States and the other nation. This can happen when the Senate approves—or ratifies—a treaty negotiated by the president to bring a conflict to an end. Congress can also **repeal**— or declare no longer effective—its declaration of war.

In 1973, Congress passed the War Powers **Resolution** to ensure that it retained the power to make decisions in matters of war and peace. The passage of this resolution was in response to the Vietnam War; Congress was trying to correct a situation in which Presidents Kennedy, Johnson, and Nixon had been allowed to commit significant numbers of American troops to an expanding war, with little success. The resolution was passed over the veto of President Nixon.

The War Powers Resolution states that the president can commit U.S. armed forces to a situation only after a declaration of war, specific authorization, or a

What was the
War Powers
Resolution?

"FREEDOM AT WAR WITH FEAR"

On the evening of September 20, 2001, nine days after terrorists attacked the United States, President George W. Bush appeared before a joint session of the House of Representatives and the Senate. His speech, entitled "Freedom at War with Fear," would rally and reassure the nation:

In the normal course of events, presidents come to this chamber to report on the state of the Union. Tonight, no such report is needed. It has already been delivered by the American people. . . .

My fellow citizens, for the last nine days, the entire world has seen for itself the state of our Union—and it is strong. . . .

Our response involves far more than instant retaliation and isolated strikes. Americans should not expect one battle, but a lengthy campaign, unlike any other we have ever seen. It may include dramatic strikes, visible on TV, and covert operations, secret even in success. We will starve terrorists of funding, turn them one against another, drive them from place to place, until there is no refuge or no rest. And we will pursue nations that provide aid or safe haven to terrorism. Every nation, in every region, now has a decision to make. Either you are with us, or you are with the terrorists. From this day forward, any nation that continues to harbor or support terrorism will be regarded by the United States as a hostile regime. . . .

After all that has just passed—all the lives taken, and all the possibilities and hopes that died with them—it is natural to wonder if America's future is one of fear. Some speak of an age of terror. I know there are struggles ahead, and dangers to face. But this country will define our times, not be defined by them. As long as the United States of America is determined and strong, this will not be an age of terror; this will be an age of liberty, here and across the world. . . .

national emergency created by an attack on the United States or its armed forces. The resolution requires the president to inform the House and Senate in writing within 48 hours of any commitment or substantial increase of U.S. combat forces abroad, and it states that the troop commitment must end within 60 days after the president's initial report is submitted unless Congress declares war, specifically approves the continued troop commitment, or is physically unable to meet because of an attack on the United States. Finally, the act also allows Congress to direct the president to remove troops from conflict anytime U.S. forces are involved in combat without a declaration of war or specific congressional approval for military action.

Veto Power

The word *veto* comes from the Latin for "I forbid." The president has the power to veto laws and acts passed by Congress, although his or her veto can be overruled if two-thirds of the members of Congress vote to do so.

According to the Constitution, when Congress passes a bill (an act of legislation) and sends it to the president, he or she has three possible responses: approve and sign the bill, making it a law; veto (or reject) the bill and return it to the House of Representatives or Senate, whichever it came from, within 10 days; or do nothing. If the president chooses to do nothing, the bill becomes law after 10 days. (If Congress sends a bill to the president and then adjourns before 10 days have passed and before the president has responded, the bill dies. This is called a *pocket veto*.)

If the president vetoes a bill, congressional actions determine what happens next. If two-thirds of the members present in both the House and Senate pass the vetoed bill, it becomes law, even though the president has vetoed it. If the House and Senate do not respond, or if not enough members vote to pass the bill, it dies. Congress can then try to rewrite the bill to make it more acceptable to the president, or give up on it.

Most early presidents used the veto power sparingly, generally only for bills that they felt were unconstitutional. Andrew Jackson was the first president to use the veto as a political weapon against his opponents in Congress. During his time in office, he issued 12 vetoes, more than any president who had come before him.

Party politics were sharp and divisive in the years after the Civil War, and the use of presidential veto power reflected this. Andrew Johnson was the first president whose veto of an important bill was overridden by Congress. In fact, Congress overturned 15 of Johnson's 21 vetoes. These divisions contributed to Johnson's impeachment by the House; he was **acquitted** in the Senate by only one vote.

President Franklin D. Roosevelt used his veto power against major tax legislation, and he also used the threat of the veto to help him maintain control of many of the laws passed during his presidency. As we read earlier, President Nixon tried

A caricature from the 1830s depicts Andrew Jackson as a tyrannical monarch, holding a scepter in one hand and a "veto" in the other. Jackson was the first president to use the veto as a political weapon against opponents in Congress.

to veto the War Powers Resolution that would have limited his ability to commit U.S. forces abroad, but his veto was overridden. The veto power becomes a political tool most often in cases where the president represents one political party, and the majority of the members in Congress are of a different political party.

The Nation's Diplomat

The Constitution grants to the president the power to make treaties (provided that two-thirds of the Senate approves). It also gives the president the power to appoint ambassadors and to receive ambassadors and **diplomats** from foreign nations.

The president is, in many ways, the most visible representative of the United States to other countries. Modern presidents travel to multiple continents during their terms in office, firming up alliances and trying to build new ones. The president is the official spokesperson for the United States and, because of the powers given to him or her in the Constitution, he or she has several different opportunities to influence foreign policy. Through his veto power, he or she can influence laws related to foreign policy passed by Congress. As commander in chief, he or she can take—or threaten—military action other than an actual declared war. With the power to appoint ambassadors, the president can choose the men and women who represent the United States overseas. With the power to "receive" (or welcome) foreign ambassadors, the president can choose which countries' representatives he or she will meet with.

George Washington used treaties rather than personal meetings or agreements with foreign leaders to shape foreign policy; he also consulted Senate leaders to obtain approval before negotiating treaties. Washington was the one who set the precedent that it would be the president who recognized foreign governments—meaning that when a new country was formed, whether through war, revolution, or overthrow of an existing government, it would be the president who formally recognizes it as a new nation. Washington also used his powers to demand that ambassadors be recalled, or sent back to their home countries, if they broke U.S. law or committed some offense.

One of Washington's more controversial foreign policy actions was his Neutrality Proclamation of 1793. In it, Washington announced publicly that the United States would remain "friendly and impartial" in the war that had erupted between France and Great Britain. In that case, Congress supported Washington's decision by passing the Neutrality Act of 1794. But many, including Secretary

President George W. Bush is shown talking with Russian President Vladimir Putin during a working session of the G8 Summit in July 2006 in St. Petersburg, Russia.

of State Thomas Jefferson, objected to Washington's actions. Their argument was that, if the power to declare war belonged to Congress, then the power to decide that the nation would not engage in war also should belong to Congress.

Presidential control over foreign policy also includes the management of the people within the executive branch whose work is related to foreign affairs. These include the employees of the State Department, the Department of Defense, the National Security Agency, the Central Intelligence Agency and all other intelligence agencies, and the Department of Homeland Security.

Political Appointments

Besides the power to appoint ambassadors and consuls, the president has the power to appoint other political officials who will make decisions and manage many different divisions of the federal government. This is a critical power, one shared to a certain extent with the Senate. The Constitution grants the president the right to name potential appointees; the Senate can either confirm or reject the candidates.

Under the Constitution, the president has the power to select all civilian employees of the federal government whose appointment is not expressly given to other branches of the government. The size of the federal government, however, has dramatically grown since the Constitution was first drafted, with about 2.6 million civilian employees. Today, staff members for the less prominent government positions are recruited and hired by the federal civil service system.

One criticism of presidential appointments is the possibility of **patronage**, or the system of giving jobs to supporters and friends. Presidential appointments are closely studied, and candidates must be prepared to defend their background, public statements, and qualifications for the job.

When a new president is elected, Congress publishes *Policy and Supporting Positions*, a book that lists the top executive branch positions available for direct presidential appointments. Many of these require Senate confirmation. In general, each new presidential administration is responsible for appointing 200 members of the White House staff, 15 department heads, about 150 ambassadors, as well as many other personnel. Out of these positions, probably about 300 "top jobs"—such as members of the president's cabinet, heads of bureaus, and undersecretaries—are of most concern to the president.

Presidents also have the power to appoint justices to the Supreme Court in the event of a vacancy during their term. This provides the president with an opportunity to influence a separate branch of government—the judicial branch—by placing on the Supreme Court a justice whose positions on legal issues closely reflect his or her own. Supreme Court justices do not serve fixed terms, nor must they step down when the president who appointed them leaves office. For this reason, Supreme Court appointments offer a president an opportunity to influence the American judicial system well after his or her administration has ended. The two most recent Supreme Court appointments occurred under the administration of President Donald Trump. In 2017, Trump appointed Neil Gorsuch following the death of Antonin Scalia, and in 2018—after a contentious confirmation process in which he faced accusations of sexual assault—Trump appointee Brett Kavanaugh was confirmed to take the place of retired justice Anthony Kennedy.

Political appointees are often selected based on their work and educational experience. Previous government service is not a requirement—in fact, many

Presidents have the power to appoint justices to the Supreme Court, giving them a chance to put their mark on the court long after their term of office has ended. President George W. Bush appointed Chief Justice John Roberts and Justice Samuel Alito. Here, Alito sits before the Senate Judiciary Committee for his confirmation hearing.

appointees have never worked in the government before. Presidents generally choose candidates who share their vision for that particular office or department and who will demonstrate loyalty to the president. Presidents will also often try to demonstrate balance in their appointments, selecting candidates from different regions of the country, for example. In recent years, presidents have used their appointments to demonstrate a commitment to gender or racial equality. President Lyndon Johnson appointed the first African American justice to the Supreme Court, Thurgood Marshall, and President Ronald Reagan appointed the first female justice, Sandra Day O'Connor. Bill Clinton appointed the first woman as secretary of state, Madeleine Albright. George W. Bush appointed the first African American secretary of state, Colin Powell, and first female African American secretary of state, Condoleezza Rice, named after Powell stepped down.

Although the president has the power to nominate appointees, the Senate retains the power to confirm major presidential appointments. Nominees must supply Senate committees with detailed financial records and undergo background checks, and nominees are often called before Senate committees to answer questions. Although the majority of presidential appointees are confirmed, the Senate does use its power to investigate presidential nominees thoroughly, and, on occasion, nominees are rejected. In recent years, nominees have often asked the president to withdraw their names if it seemed likely that the Senate would not confirm them. The Senate may also use its power to confirm presidential appointments as a negotiating tool to seek presidential support for other policies.

Other Presidential Powers

The president has several powers that are not specifically mentioned in the Constitution but are nonetheless critical to the president's role as the country's chief executive. He or she plays a vital role in the shaping of the national budget, often deciding where and how money will be spent. While Congress controls national spending, it is the president who prepares and submits a budget for congressional approval.

The president also has the responsibility to ensure that "the Laws be faithfully executed," meaning that he or she must act as the nation's chief law enforcement official. President John F. Kennedy used this power to order U.S. marshals (and later federal troops) to Oxford, Mississippi, to provide federal support for a court order requiring the University of Mississippi to enroll an African American student, James Meredith, in 1962. The marshals and troops were sent to maintain order on the campus and to protect Meredith.

The law enforcement power also places the president at the head of federal law enforcement agencies, including the Federal Bureau of Investigation, the Office of Citizenship and Immigration Services, the Drug Enforcement Administration, and the U.S. Marshals Service. The Justice Department is the president's principal law enforcement agency. Investigations and law enforcement also may be carried out by the Food and Drug Administration, U.S. Customs and Border Protection, the Secret Service, and the Internal Revenue Service. Other areas of federal law enforcement are carried out by the Department of Labor, the Occupational Safety and Health Administration, the Federal Aviation Administration, and the Coast Guard.

Text-Dependent Questions

1. Why did Congress pass the War Powers Resolution in 1973?

2. When Congress passes a bill and sends it to the president, what are the president's three possible responses?

3. What is *Policy and Supporting Positions*, and when is it published?

Research Project

Research three of the positions a president has the power to fill, including heads of federal executive departments, White House staff members, ambassadors, justices of the Supreme Court, and federal judges. Write a brief report outlining the duties and responsibilities of each of the three positions, with biographical information on the current appointee.

Inside the Oval Office

The Oval Office is the president's office, and when he or she is at the White House, it is the heart of presidential business. The Oval Office is not a historic part of the presidency—in fact, the entire West Wing of the White House, where the Oval Office is located, is little more than 100 years old.

It was Washington who began the practice of holding gatherings in an oval room. In his home in Philadelphia, where the capital was then located, Washington altered two rooms to make them oval, and he would hold formal receptions there. Washington would stand in the center of the room, with guests gathered around him in a circle. The idea was to ensure that there was no top or bottom, no head or foot, to the room, so that everyone could be an equal distance from the president.

John Adams was the first president to occupy the White House, at the time called the "President's House," when the capital relocated to Washington, D.C., from Philadelphia. The building was not finished when Adams moved into it in 1800. Thirteen fires had to be kept burning constantly to

After a president takes office, he or she lives in the White House and works in the Oval Office. Each president has the opportunity to decorate the office, too. Pictured here is the office as it looked under President Bill Clinton.

help speed up the drying of paint and plaster, and only six of the building's 30 rooms were completed. Adams's wife, Abigail, hung her laundry to dry in the large, unfinished reception room.

For many years, presidents lived and worked on the second floor of the White House. President Theodore Roosevelt, however, found the living quarters on the second floor too cramped for his large family, and he decided to have new working space built in a separate building on the west side of the White House. At the time, the White House's greenhouses were in that area, but in 1902 they were moved to make way for the new office space.

The Oval Office in the West Wing was the idea of President William Howard Taft, who in 1909 decided that the president's office should be in the center of the West Wing. Taft wanted to ensure that the president was at the center of all West Wing operations and involved in all of the day-to-day activities of the presidency. The Oval Office was moved to its current location—next to the Rose Garden—under President Franklin D. Roosevelt.

In many ways, the Oval Office has become a symbol of the American presidency. Photos of the president frequently show the Oval Office; the president may deliver important speeches from behind his or her desk in the Oval Office.

President George W. Bush held a meeting on December 20, 2001, in the Oval Office, which was decorated with the new presidential rug that had arrived earlier in the week. Presidents choose the design for the rug in the Oval Office, though all rugs feature the Great Seal of the United States in the center.

Tradition dictates that each president chooses the decor of the Oval Office, and interesting glimpses into the presidential character—into the people he admired and his vision for the country—can be seen in how he or she chooses to decorate his office. President Taft's Oval Office was decorated in olive green, with caribou hides tacked with gold studs on the chairs, and a wooden floor with a checkerboard pattern.

In more recent years, the floor of the Oval Office has been covered with a large rug, whose design has been chosen by each president. President George W. Bush chose a sunny, optimistic yellow to decorate the Oval Office, with a rug designed to mimic the sunlight flowing in through the large windows looking out onto the South Lawn of the White House. The presidential rugs all feature the Great Seal of the United States in their center. The eagle depicted holds an olive branch in one of its talons and several arrows in the other. Today, the eagle's head is turned toward the olive branch, although it used to face the arrows. This change was made by President Harry Truman after World War II, to demonstrate that the United States would now be looking toward peace rather than war.

The desk in the Oval Office is also chosen by the president. Many recent presidents have selected the desk known as "HMS *Resolute*," including Theodore and Franklin D. Roosevelt, Ronald Reagan, Bill Clinton, and John F. Kennedy. The desk, a

President Barack Obama sits at his desk, known as the HMS Resolute, *in the Oval Office. HMS* Resolute *has been used by many presidents, including Ronald Reagan and John F. Kennedy.*

gift from Queen Victoria to President Rutherford Hayes in 1879, was made of timbers from the British ship HMS *Resolute*. This desk had originally been open in the front, but a panel was added by Franklin D. Roosevelt to hide the fact that his legs were crippled by polio.

The artwork in the Oval Office also reflects the spirit and focus of the person whose office it has become. Presidents often choose portraits or busts of former presidents whose leadership inspires them.

These items are what a visitor to the Oval Office might see. But more important than the look of the Oval Office is the work conducted there.

The President's Men and Women

The tradition of selecting a "cabinet," or collection of advisors, dates back to the very first president. George Washington's cabinet included Secretary of the Treasury Alexander Hamilton, Secretary of State Thomas Jefferson, Attorney General Edmund Randolph, and Secretary of War Henry Knox. They, along with Vice President John Adams, formed the entire cabinet 1789.

Today, the president's cabinet has considerably expanded. Presidents choose the men and women who will serve in their cabinet, based upon the approval of the Senate, and are given the opportunity to add new positions. The modern presidential cabinet includes the attorney general (who is the head of the Department of Justice) and the heads of 14 other departments: Agriculture, Commerce, Defense, Education, Energy, Health and Human Services, Homeland Security, Housing and Urban Development, Interior, Labor, State, Transportation, Treasury, and Veterans Affairs.

In addition to these permanent cabinet members, other positions are considered to be "cabinet level." President Donald Trump's cabinet includes eight such positions: the White House chief of staff, the administrator of the Environmental Protection Agency, the director of the Office of Management and Budget, the U.S. trade representative, the U.S. mission to the United Nations, the administrator of Small Business Administration, the director of the Central Intelligence Agency, and the director of National Intelligence.

Because the federal government has grown so large, and its responsibilities so vast, the president must in many ways act as a kind of chief administrator, directing the activities of the various departments through his or her instructions to the cabinet members. For this reason, the cabinet members may offer the president advice or make recommendations, but they serve at the president's request and are expected to carry out his or her programs or orders.

The president cannot possibly know every detail of what goes on in each office within the executive branch. He may have a broad vision for that office—for example, he may have an idea of how he wants the secretary of state to respond to a particular incident in a foreign country—but in essence a key to a successful presidency involves skilled **delegation**. The president is, in many ways, a manager, and successful presidents choose skilled men and women to serve them and wisely delegate enough so that they can focus and concentrate on their priorities as president.

The Communicator

The president relies on the heads of departments, and on his staff, to keep him informed of developments critical to his administration and to the nation's security and stability. It is the president, however, who is the chief communicator for his administration; he is periodically expected to communicate his policies and decisions to Congress and to the nation.

President George W. Bush delivers his State of the Union on January 31, 2006. The State of the Union speech has become a ceremonial event for presidents and Congress.

The Constitution provides for the president to "from time to time give to the Congress Information of the State of the Union." The State of the Union speech has become an annual event, giving the president the opportunity to address the Congress (and the American public, since the speeches are generally televised) and to outline the broad plans for the future, as well as to review what has been accomplished in the last 12 months.

The custom of appearing in person before the Congress to inform its members of the "State of the Union" began with George Washington and was continued by John Adams, both of whom appeared each year to deliver a message in person to Congress. Thomas Jefferson, believing this practice had too much in common with the custom of the British Parliament beginning its session with a speech from the king or queen, decided to put a stop to it. He preferred to submit his reports to Congress in writing.

Jefferson's custom of a written "State of the Union" report was continued until 1913, when Woodrow Wilson personally appeared before Congress to deliver a special speech on finance. This marked not only a return to the personal delivery of the State of the Union report in a speech, but also the beginning of the use of the speech as a way to **publicize** the president's plans and agenda. This idea became more pronounced when the speeches were broadcast on radio and, of course, on television.

Presidents have used the State of the Union speech to bring new ideas and programs to the public's attention. President Kennedy used his State of the Union speech to urge support for the effort to put a man on the moon before the end of the 1960s. Lyndon Johnson used his State of the Union speeches to urge passage of his civil rights programs, while President Nixon used his to try to gain public support for U.S. actions in Vietnam.

The State of the Union speech has become a ceremonial event for the presidency and for Congress. Among those in the audience are members of the **Joint Chiefs of Staff**, the president's cabinet, justices of the Supreme Court, and certain invited guests. Presidents may use the speech to recognize a private individual for some heroic act, to remind the audience of successful accomplishments, and to gain support for their political party.

 Watch a State of the Union address.

Through the years, presidents have used other tools to communicate their proposals and agendas. The presidential staff normally includes several speechwriters and a press secretary, who provides reporters with daily briefings, advance texts and reports, and announcements of the president's schedule and new policies.

Presidents may hold periodic news conferences to make policy announcements and answer reporters' questions. This custom began with Woodrow Wilson, who was the first president to invite reporters to his office for a question-and-answer session. Before this, presidents had usually granted interviews only to certain reporters, generally those who would report favorably on the administration. Franklin D. Roosevelt proved a master at press conferences, often holding them twice a week and entertaining reporters with his lively responses and charm. Dwight Eisenhower was the first to allow his news conferences to be televised, although he reserved the right to edit them before they were presented to the public. Under his successor, John F. Kennedy, the press conferences were no longer edited.

Presidents engage in extensive preparation before press conferences, working with their staff to guess which questions will be asked and to prepare careful responses. The frequency of presidential news conferences can reflect the president's ease at dealing with unanticipated questions or a possibly hostile questioner, and when administrations are dealing with crises, the number of press conferences often dwindles.

In the age of social media, presidents can now take to Twitter, Facebook, and other platforms to get their message across. President Donald Trump is notorious for tweeting his policies, opinions, and criticisms of rivals, with streams of dispatches

Journalists peppering President Franklin D. Roosevelt with questions during a news conference in 1943. Roosevelt proved to be a master of the news conference, often holding them twice a week.

THE "GREAT SOCIETY" SPEECH

It is the responsibility of each president to critically examine the country he leads, to carefully measure its strengths and weaknesses, and to provide leadership that will inspire. In 1964, President Lyndon Johnson chose a theme for his administration: the "Great Society." Johnson communicated this new plan for the nation at a May 1964 commencement address at the University of Michigan:

. . . The purpose of protecting the life of our nation and preserving the liberty of our citizens is to pursue the happiness of our people. Our success in that pursuit is the test of our success as a nation. For a century we labored to settle and to subdue a continent. For half a century, we called upon unbounded invention and untiring industry to create an order of plenty for all of our people. The challenge of the next half century is whether we have the wisdom to use that wealth to enrich and elevate our national life, and to advance the quality of our American civilization.

Your imagination, your initiative, and your indignation will determine whether we build a society where progress is the servant of our needs, or a society where old values and new visions are buried under unbridled growth.

For in your time we have the opportunity to move not only toward the rich society and the powerful society, but upward to the Great Society. The Great Society rests on abundance and liberty for all. It demands an end to poverty and racial injustice, to which we are totally committed in our time. But that is just the beginning.

The Great Society is a place where every child can find knowledge to enrich his mind and to enlarge his talents. It is a place where leisure is a welcome chance to build and reflect, not a feared cause of boredom and restlessness. It is a place where the city of man serves not only the needs of the body and the demands of commerce, but the desire for beauty and the hunger for community.

It is a place where man can renew contact with nature. It is a place which honors creation for its own sake and for what it adds to the understanding of the race. It is a place where men are more concerned with the quality of their goals than the quantity of their goods. But most of all, the Great Society is not a safe harbor, a resting place, a final objective, a finished work. It is a challenge constantly renewed, beckoning us toward a destiny where the meaning of our lives matches the marvelous products of our labor. . . .

arriving daily. Recent presidential campaigns, such as Bernie Sanders's bid for the Democratic Party nomination in 2016, have been fueled by social media outreach, online fundraising efforts, and email lists that build strong networks of supporters.

Instead, presidents may rely on more structured opportunities to present their policies to the public. They may make speeches before carefully screened audiences; they may give televised "addresses" or speeches during which reporters do not have an opportunity to ask questions; or they may grant interviews only to reporters with whom they have established a friendly relationship.

Text-Dependent Questions

1. What was George Washington's reasoning for making a reception room oval?

2. Which president used his State of the Union address to advocate for civil rights?

3. Who was the first president to allow his news conferences to be televised?

Research Project

Find footage of a presidential press conference, State of the Union address, or other public appearance, either via livestream on a news Web site or archived on YouTube. Take notes on the event, being sure to note the date, the purpose, the questions asked, and the president's responses. Write a brief report about the event, including your personal interpretation of how well the president conveyed his message, effective uses of language or rhetoric, and other observations.

5

Electing the President

The details of the election of a president, and how he or she leaves office, are spelled out in the Constitution. The Framers of the Constitution, though, could not have imagined the wild excesses of presidential campaigns or the many variables that have led to a president leaving office.

In the very first election, George Washington was the unanimous choice of the electors. Each elector had to name two choices on the ballot for president, and each gave one of his votes to Washington. At the time, the candidate who came in second became vice president. In that first election, John Adams became vice president.

In the future, such agreement in the choice of president would prove rare. In the early years of the United States, men who were instrumental in the shaping of the new nation's government would become its leaders—men like Washington, Adams, Thomas Jefferson, and James Madison. Future

The U.S. presidential election starts with a campaign and ends with Inauguration Day. Each candidate must fight for the respect and support from their peers and the American people.

generations, though, would need to find other ways to select the man (for until now it has always been a man) who would become president. And the process of choosing a president would become increasingly complex.

The Electoral College

When creating the Constitution, the delegates to the Constitutional Convention considered several ways to elect a president. They considered and rejected the idea that Congress would choose the president. They considered and rejected the idea that the legislatures of each state would choose the president. They also considered and rejected the idea that a president would be directly elected by the people. The problems with the first two options are clear, but why did the Framers of the Constitution reject the last option?

It is important to remember that, at the time, the population of the 13 states was widely scattered, and there were no quick means of communication connecting the states. The delegates feared that the voters would not easily be able to find out much information about the different candidates for the presidency. Without this kind of information, they would probably vote for the candidate with whom they were familiar, most likely the one from their state or region. That would give an advantage to candidates from the more heavily populated and larger states.

To create a more balanced system, the Framers of the Constitution came up with the idea of an "Electoral College." The idea was that well-informed people would be selected from each state to cast their vote for the best presidential candidate. The number of voters, or delegates to the Electoral College, is based on the number of congressional representatives each state has. So, clearly there is an advantage for larger, more populated states, which will have more votes to cast in the Electoral College.

The Constitution contains the details of what would become the first Electoral College. In it, each state was given two electoral votes (one for each senator) plus one vote for each member of the House of Representatives. Each state could decide how its electors would be chosen, but congressmen and employees of the federal government could not serve as electors. Each elector had to cast two votes for president, and one of those votes had to be for someone who was not from their home state. The person with the most electoral votes (and it had to be more than one-half of the votes) would become president. If no one received more than half of the votes, or if there was a tie, the election would be decided by the House of Representatives. Members of the House would review the top five candidates, and each state would be allowed to cast only one vote. The president would need to receive more than half of all the votes cast.

This system worked for only four presidential elections. In the election of 1800, Thomas Jefferson and Aaron Burr received an equal number of votes. It took many days and 36 separate voting sessions (plus a lot of behind-the-scenes deal-making) before the House of Representatives finally resolved the election in favor of Jefferson.

This led to the ratification of the Twelfth Amendment to the Constitution in 1804. The rules were changed so that each elector would cast one vote for president and a separate vote for vice president, rather than the previous system of casting two votes for president. According to the amendment, if no one receives more than half of the votes, then the House of Representatives chooses the president from the top three contenders, with each state casting only one vote. The amendment also specified that either the president or vice president had to be from a state other than that of the electors. This is why modern presidential and vice-presidential candidates are always from different states.

Today, most states choose their electors by statewide election. Most follow a "winner take all" system. This means that the presidential candidate who wins the popular vote in a state receives all of that state's electors. It is interesting to note that when a citizen casts their vote in a presidential election, they are not directly voting for that presidential candidate, but instead for the *electors* for the presidential candidate they have chosen.

During the first presidential elections, states were given the right to choose their electors on whatever date they fixed. In 1845, Congress passed a law specifying that all states would choose their electors on the same day—the Tuesday following the first Monday in November in years that can be divided by four. That day remains the day on which presidential elections are held.

Problems with Electing the President

The election of 1800 was not the only time that the system devised for choosing a president caused trouble. In 1824, the electoral votes were split among four strong candidates—John Quincy Adams, Andrew Jackson, Henry Clay, and

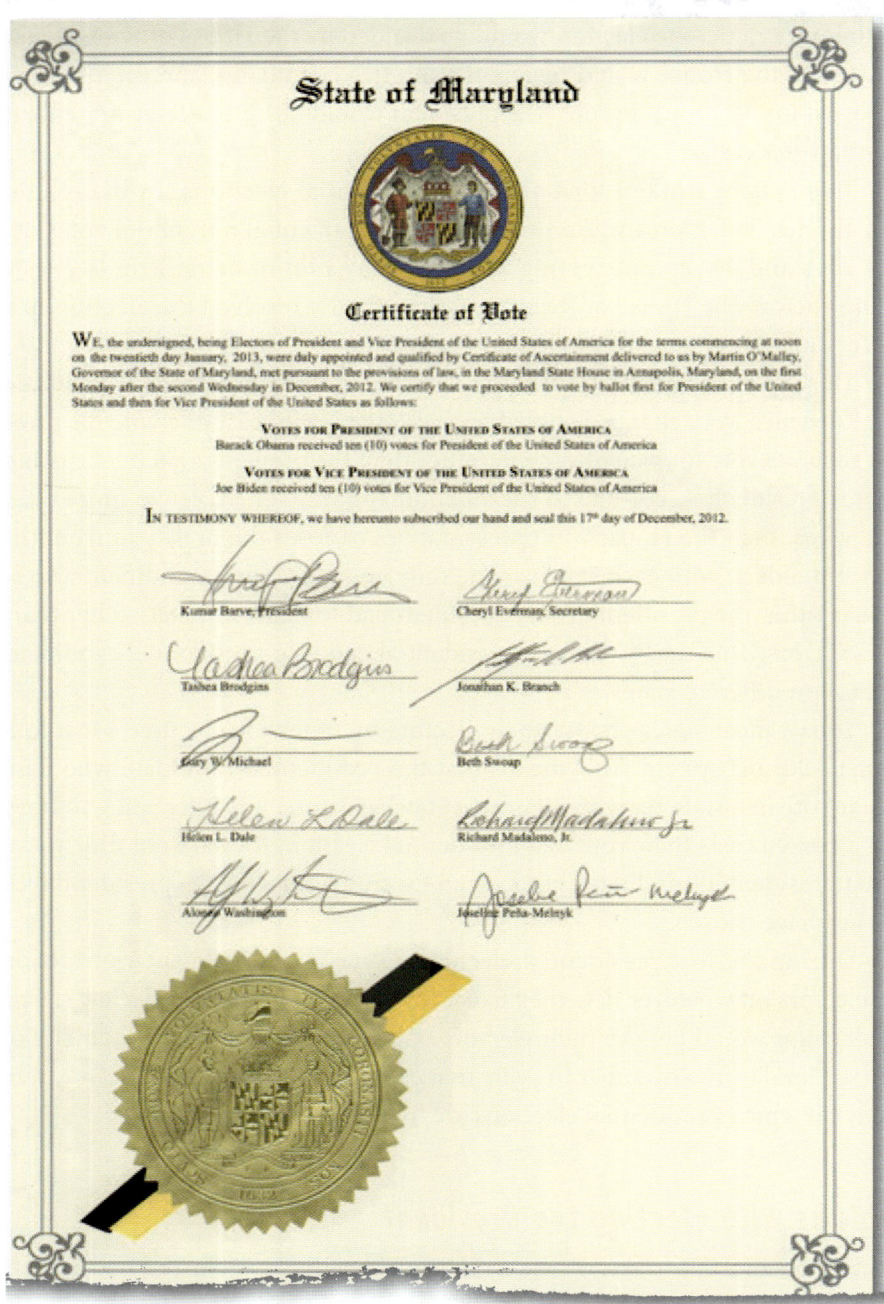

State of Maryland

Certificate of Vote

WE, the undersigned, being Electors of President and Vice President of the United States of America for the terms commencing at noon on the twentieth day January, 2013, were duly appointed and qualified by Certificate of Ascertainment delivered to us by Martin O'Malley, Governor of the State of Maryland, met pursuant to the provisions of law, in the Maryland State House in Annapolis, Maryland, on the first Monday after the second Wednesday in December, 2012. We certify that we proceeded to vote by ballot first for President of the United States and then for Vice President of the United States as follows:

VOTES FOR PRESIDENT OF THE UNITED STATES OF AMERICA
Barack Obama received ten (10) votes for President of the United States of America

VOTES FOR VICE PRESIDENT OF THE UNITED STATES OF AMERICA
Joe Biden received ten (10) votes for Vice President of the United States of America

IN TESTIMONY WHEREOF, we have hereunto subscribed our hand and seal this 17th day of December, 2012.

Kumar Barve, President   Cheryl Everman, Secretary

Tashea Brodgins   Jonathan K. Branch

Gary W. Michael   Beth Swoop

Helen L. Dale   Richard Madaleno, Jr.

Alonzo Washington   Joseline Peña-Melnyk

Each state has a group of electors. Pictured here is a certificate of vote from the state of Maryland in the 2012 election. The electors chose Barack Obama and Joe Biden.

CAMP DAVID

Presidents seeking a retreat from the White House, and a more informal setting at which to relax and meet with staff members or guests, can travel to Camp David, some 70 miles from Washington in the Catoctin Mountains of Maryland.

President Franklin D. Roosevelt first established Camp David on the site of a camp for federal workers and their families. He drew up the plans for the construction of a main lodge and improvements to many of the cabins on the grounds; he called it "Shangri-La" and was the first president to use the camp during a three-day retreat in 1942. He also played host to the first foreign official there—Prime Minister Winston Churchill of Great Britain in 1943.

President Dwight Eisenhower renamed the retreat Camp David in honor of his grandson, David Eisenhower. Eisenhower held the first cabinet meeting at Camp David.

The retreat has served as the site of important meetings and summits. In 1978, President Jimmy Carter conducted Middle East peace negotiations with Israel's Menachem Begin and Egypt's Anwar Sadat in what became known as the Camp David Accords.

President Ronald Reagan spent more time at Camp David than any other president. President George H.W. Bush's daughter, Dorothy, was married there. Besides privacy and cooler temperatures, Camp David offers a pool, a putting green, a driving range, tennis courts, and a workout center. The president normally travels to Camp David by helicopter.

William Crawford. No one received a clear majority (more than half) of the votes, and it fell to the House of Representatives to choose the president. Andrew Jackson had received more electoral votes than any of the other three contenders, but the House narrowly selected John Quincy Adams as president.

In 1876, the election was between Samuel Tilden and Rutherford Hayes. Most counts showed that Tilden had won the majority of the popular vote, but the electoral votes in South Carolina, Louisiana, and Florida were in question. In the end, each state provided two sets of electoral votes, one for Tilden and one for Hayes. Congress appointed a 15-member commission to decide the electoral votes in each of the three states. There were charges of making political deals and behind-the-scenes negotiations, but in the end the commission narrowly chose Hayes as the winner of the electoral votes in each of the three states, and he was elected president. In 1887, Congress passed a law giving each state the final authority to determine whether its electoral votes were legal.

In 1888, the election between Benjamin Harrison and Grover Cleveland demonstrated how a candidate could win the popular vote and still lose the election. Benjamin Harrison, the Republican candidate, barely won majorities in some of the larger of the 20 states that supported him, while Cleveland won huge majorities of the popular vote in the 18 states that supported him. In the overall popular vote, Cleveland surpassed Harrison 5,534,488 to 5,443,892. Nonetheless, the candidate who won the majority of electoral votes—in this case, Benjamin Harrison (233 to 168)—was elected president.

In more recent history, the 2000 presidential election demonstrated the significance of electoral votes in one of the closest elections in history. On election night, many television networks prematurely announced a winner in the election before it was decided that the results were too close to call. The election came down to the 25 electoral votes of the state of Florida. When it was learned that Republican candidate George W. Bush had won by only a little more than 1,000 votes in Florida over Democratic challenger Al Gore, a **recount** of the votes was ordered. It took nearly a month of court challenges and recounts before the U.S. Supreme Court finally intervened, stating that each Florida county was using different vote-counting standards and there was insufficient time to create a single standard and appoint an impartial official to oversee the recounts. The election was awarded to George W. Bush; the disputed final results show Bush winning Florida's electors by only 537 votes.

News footage from the 2000 election.

Primaries and Caucuses

The creation of political parties and the vast media attention devoted to presidential elections has transformed the process of choosing the president. Today, candidates must raise vast amounts of money to support a political campaign, and the process of attracting public attention (and campaign contributions) begins well before the national election. Generally, candidates declare their intention to run for the presidency at least a year before the national election is held.

The first goal that candidates face is to win their political party's nomination for the general election at a nominating convention held the summer before the general election. To become the Democratic or Republican candidate for president, a candidate must be nominated at the Democratic Party's or the Republican Party's convention. Since there may be more than one candidate from the party seeking to become president, **primaries** and **caucuses** are held to give voters the opportunity to register their support for a particular candidate before the nominating convention is held.

Primaries began in the early part of the twentieth century. Before this, candidates for each party were, for the most part, chosen by party insiders, who made deals and traded favors while selecting the candidate they thought would be most likely to win a presidential election.

In some states, only voters who are registered to a particular party can vote for that party's candidate in a primary—for example, only registered Republicans can vote for the Republican candidate. In other states, voters can vote for another party's candidate.

The nomination of presidential candidates generally involves either primaries or caucuses, depending on the state's rules. A primary resembles a general election—voters go to a polling place and cast their vote for a particular candidate. In a caucus, party members gather together in a public place and often listen to speeches before casting their votes for delegates to represent a particular candidate at the party's national convention.

Within each state, Republican and Democratic primaries and caucuses are held at the same time, but the dates when these votes occur vary from state to state. This happens between January and June of an election year. One criticism of this system is that states that hold the first primaries and caucuses—Iowa and New Hampshire—receive a large amount of attention from the candidates and the

John Kerry at a caucus site in Des Moines, Iowa, in January 2004. Primaries and caucuses are held to give voters the chance to choose who they want to run for president as the Republican or Democratic nominee.

media—attention that does not necessarily reflect the number of electoral votes they will ultimately cast for president. Candidates who do not perform well in the earlier primaries and caucuses may have to drop out before the primaries and caucuses have ended, meaning that states that hold their primaries and caucuses first have a greater opportunity to influence the ultimate choice of presidential candidate. Many states, including New York, Ohio, and California (with large numbers of electoral votes), hold their primaries on the same Tuesday in March, which has become known as "Super Tuesday."

The primaries and caucuses decide how many delegates for each candidate will be sent to the national convention. At the national convention, the delegates from each state then vote for the candidate they wish to receive the party's nomination. The winner is selected as the party's official candidate for president.

The Campaign

Once the parties have chosen their candidates for president, these nominees spend the next several months demonstrating to the voters why they would be the best president. In the country's early years, many candidates believed that it was undignified to express an interest in becoming president. They felt that they should seem to be above the election process, leaving the campaigning and negotiations to their supporters.

The campaign provides an opportunity to present the candidate to the voters, highlighting certain strengths and types of experience, and focusing on specific issues. Throughout the years, campaigns have highlighted the candidates' positions on the economy, defense, civil rights, and a wide range of other issues that reflect the concerns of voters at a particular time.

Campaigns have traditionally not only highlighted a particular candidate's strengths but also an opponent's weaknesses. Even candidates like John Adams and Thomas Jefferson inspired fierce criticism. In the 1800 presidential election, voters were warned of the dangers of re-electing Adams with posters that proclaimed, "REPUBLICANS, Turn out, turn out and save your Country from ruin!"

Campaigns frequently focus on a candidate's background. In the nineteenth century, a candidate's humble beginnings were considered an asset, and many presidential candidates emphasized their births in log cabins and their time spent on the frontier. Campaigns might emphasize a candidate's war service or his political experience, or link him to other popular figures. In recent years, it has been considered a liability, rather than an asset, to have spent too much of a career in Washington, and candidates who have served as U.S. senators or representatives will frequently have their campaigns focus on other aspects of their background.

Television has also dramatically changed the presidential campaign process. Now campaigns focus on televised appearances by the candidate to present a particular issue or position to the voters. Appearance matters—candidates who appear poised and confident in front of the cameras are much more likely to win the election. This was first proved in the 1960 presidential election, the first in which debates between the two presidential candidates were televised. Polls showed that voters who had listened to the debates on the radio thought that Republican candidate Richard Nixon had won, but television viewers strongly favored Democratic candidate John F. Kennedy, who appeared relaxed, attractive, and confident on camera. Kennedy ultimately won the presidential election.

Presidential debates were first televised in 1960, when John F. Kennedy and Richard Nixon were running for president.

Today, candidates must face a twenty-four-hour news cycle in which every word, gesture, and action is analyzed and picked apart by commentators. The smallest misstep on the campaign trail might become a full-blown news story for a couple of hours, only to die down the following day. Candidates must also engage with social media networks if they hope to attract a following. Facebook pages, Twitter feeds, and Instagram profiles are expected tools of the political trade. At times it seems as if the "public square"—that place where citizens gather to debate and discuss the best ways forward for the country—has moved online. Through the connective world of the Internet, candidates and their supporters raise funds, recruit volunteers, and challenge the ideas of their opponents, sometimes directly.

Text-Dependent Questions

1. What was the purpose of the Twelfth Amendment to the Constitution?

2. Who were the two candidates in the contested election of 1876?

3. When was the first presidential election in which debates between the two candidates were televised?

Research Project

Research the Internet presence of the current president or a presidential candidate, including official Web sites, social media accounts, and You-Tube channels and videos. How is the president or candidate using the Internet to communicate his or her message? What are some unifying themes of this message? Is there a particular tone or type of language used, and if so, how would you describe it? Do supporters appear to be engaged? Write a brief report that answers these questions. Include your opinion on the effectiveness of the president or candidate's Internet outreach.

Presidential Transitions

In most cases, a candidate becomes president after an election. There is an orderly transition after four or eight years (depending on whether a president is re-elected).

There have been occasions, however, when a president was unable to serve his full term. Presidents have died after illnesses, have been killed, and have resigned.

There is a specific plan in place should the president be unable to complete his term in office. The order of who succeeds the president has changed over the years. The order of succession spelled out in the Presidential Succession Act of 1947, signed by President Harry Truman, is still in effect today.

Should the president be unable to complete his term, he will be succeeded by the vice president. If the vice president is also unable to serve, people in the following offices (in this order) will become president, provided that they meet the constitutional requirements for the presidency (at least 35 years old, a natural-born citizen of the United States, and a U.S. resident for at least 14 years): the Speaker of the House, president **pro tempore** of the Senate (the senator who presides over the Senate when the vice president

"Air Force One" is the call sign for any aircraft transporting the president of the United States.

is absent), secretary of state, secretary of the treasury, secretary of defense, attorney general, secretary of the interior, secretary of agriculture, secretary of commerce, secretary of labor, secretary of health and human services, secretary of housing and urban development, secretary of transportation, secretary of energy, secretary of education, secretary of veterans affairs, and secretary of homeland security.

Death in Office

A president has died in office after an illness four times. The shortest presidential term in history was that of William Henry Harrison, who died in 1841, only one month after becoming president. Harrison was 68 years old, but many suggest that his inaugural address was to blame for his death. The day of his inauguration was bitterly cold, and Harrison was outside for nearly two hours delivering the longest inaugural speech in history. He caught a cold, which developed into pneumonia, and he died.

Zachary Taylor served from 1849 to 1850. He became ill after participating in a ceremony on a blisteringly hot July 4 at the Washington Monument, which was still under construction. Within five days, he was dead, succeeded by Millard Fillmore.

William Henry Harrison, who died just a month after his inauguration, had the shortest presidency on record. He is also known, however, for giving the longest inaugural address in history.

Warren Harding served from 1921 to 1923. Corruption and scandals had already weakened his administration when Harding set out on a western tour in the summer of 1923. He collapsed in San Francisco and died of a heart attack.

Franklin D. Roosevelt remains the longest-serving president. He was elected to four terms but died before completing his last term. Roosevelt served from 1933 to 1945. His health had been poor for many of his last years in office, and he died of a brain hemorrhage on April 12, 1945.

Assassinations

As a public symbol of the United States, the president receives tremendous attention. Presidents inspire strong emotions, both admiration and hatred. It is perhaps not surprising that presidents may become targets for attack. The **Secret Service** is charged with protecting the president and his or her family from these attacks, but assassination attempts have been made on several presidents. In four cases, presidents were killed.

Presidents Andrew Jackson, Theodore Roosevelt, Franklin Roosevelt, Harry Truman, Gerald Ford, and Ronald Reagan were the victims of attempted assassinations. In Jackson's case, the guns misfired. Theodore Roosevelt and Reagan were wounded but survived. In Franklin Roosevelt's case, the bullets missed him but killed the mayor of Chicago and wounded several other people. Similarly, the attempt on Truman left him unhurt, but a guard died, and two others were wounded. Gerald Ford survived two assassination attempts within a three-week period. No one was injured in the attempts.

President Abraham Lincoln was the first president to be assassinated while in office. Lincoln died on April 15, 1865, after being shot by John Wilkes Booth while attending a performance at Ford's Theatre in Washington.

President James Garfield was shot on July 2, 1881, at a Washington railroad station by an attorney who had unsuccessfully sought a diplomatic position. Garfield lay wounded at the White House for several weeks and then was moved to the New Jersey coast. It was probably poor medical care that contributed to Garfield's death—he died on September 19, 1881, from an infection and internal bleeding.

William McKinley served as president from 1897 to 1901. He was shot by a crazed opponent of his policies while standing in a receiving line in Buffalo and died eight days later.

Hours after the assassination of President John F. Kennedy, Vice President Lyndon B. Johnson was sworn in aboard Air Force One with Jackie Kennedy by his side.

President John F. Kennedy was also the victim of assassination. He was shot and killed on November 22, 1963, while traveling in a motorcade through the streets of Dallas, Texas.

Impeachment

The Constitution specifies that presidents can face impeachment and be removed from office if they are convicted of "**Treason**, Bribery, or other high Crimes and Misdemeanors." Only two presidents have undergone impeachment trials: Andrew Johnson in 1868 and Bill Clinton in 1999.

In order for a president to be removed from office, there must first be a formal accusation in the House of Representatives and then an impeachment trial and conviction in the Senate. A majority vote (more than half of the votes) is required for the House to order an impeachment, but a two-thirds majority is necessary for the

In this photo from the U.S. Senate, Chief Justice William H. Rehnquist swears in President Bill Clinton in Washington, D.C., at the 1993 inauguration. Six years later, Rehnquist would swear in the U.S. senators as jurors in January 1999 in Clinton's impeachment trial. A two-thirds majority of senators must vote to convict in an impeachment trial; Clinton was not convicted.

AIR FORCE ONE

The presidential transportation known as Air Force One is actually two planes: specially designed Boeing 747 aircraft that are capable of flying halfway around the world without refueling and can accommodate up to 70 passengers. When the president is aboard either plane—or any Air Force aircraft—its call sign automatically becomes "Air Force One."

President Franklin D. Roosevelt was the first to call for the creation of what became known as the Presidential Pilot Office to provide air transportation for the president and his staff in 1944. The first jet aircraft—a Boeing 707—was purchased in 1962.

Air Force One functions as a traveling office for the president and his or her staff. Onboard, they have access to secure phone, fax, and computer lines, as well as copiers and printers. The president has his or her own office onboard, as well as a bedroom, a bathroom, and a dining room that is also used as a conference room. Senior staff members have their own office space, and there is a separate seating area for reporters traveling with the president.

A crew of 26 people serves onboard Air Force One. Because the two Air Force One jets are military aircraft, they are built to withstand air attacks. They also have in-flight refueling connections; the jets do not need to land to refuel.

Richard Nixon resigned from office on August 9, 1974, to avoid an impeachment trial in which he would probably have been convicted.

Senate to convict a president. In the event of an impeachment trial, the chief justice of the Supreme Court presides over the Senate.

In the cases of Johnson and Clinton, there were not enough votes to convict in the Senate. Both men remained in office.

Richard Nixon announces his resignation.

Resignation

President Richard Nixon was the first and only president to resign his office. Nixon resigned to avoid facing an impeachment trial, which probably would have resulted in his conviction.

Shortly after Nixon's re-election in 1972, his administration became involved in the Watergate scandal, which involved a break-in at the offices of the Democratic

National Committee at the Watergate hotel complex. The break-in was traced to members of Nixon's re-election committee. Ultimately, it was revealed that Nixon had known of the involvement and had tried to cover it up. Nixon resigned on August 9, 1974, and was succeeded by Gerald Ford.

Ford had been appointed by Nixon in 1973, after the resignation of Nixon's first vice president, Spiro Agnew. Upon becoming president, Ford appointed Nelson Rockefeller as his vice president. For the 29 months that Ford served as president, the country was run by a president and vice president who had not been elected to the offices they held.

Text-Dependent Questions

1. Who held the shortest presidential term in history?

2. Which two presidents have undergone impeachment trials?

3. Why did Richard Nixon resign?

Research Projects

1. Research one of the two impeachment trials in U.S. presidential history. Find out the historical background of the trial, the reasons for impeachment, how the trial played out in the House and Senate, and the president's and public's reactions. Write a brief report summarizing your findings.

2. Research the Watergate scandal that nearly resulted in the impeachment trial of Richard Nixon. Look up key figures and events, Nixon's motivations for his involvement and subsequent cover-up, and other information. Write a brief report that includes information about how the scandal impacted the country and the office of the presidency.

Who Wants to Be President?

Words to Understand

Cabinet officers: Advisers to the president whose senior members include the vice president and heads of the federal executive departments.

Plantation: Estate on which crops, such as sugar, tobacco, coffee, and cotton are tended by resident labor, such as slaves.

Territories: Areas administered by the United States government that are not recognized as states.

*H*ELP WANTED *for senior government position. Must be willing to undergo rigorous screening process and challenging campaign season. Must be able to commit to position for at least four years, with possibility of additional four years. Successful candidate must be at least 35 years old, a U.S. citizen, and have lived in the country for at least 14 years. Military service and fundraising skills helpful, but not required.*

Responsibilities include: representing country at home and overseas; meeting with major world leaders; negotiating treaties; shaping policy; serving as commander in chief of the armed forces; preparing annual budget; appointing ambassadors, justices of the Supreme Court, and other specified public officials. Must prepare annual progress report to be delivered to Congress.

George Washington, Thomas Jefferson, Theodore Roosevelt, and Abraham Lincoln are carved in to Mount Rushmore in South Dakota. The designer, Gutzon Borglum, chose these four presidents because he believed they represented the most important events in U.S. history.

Benefits include housing and transportation, bodyguards for personal protection, plus use of jet, vacation retreat, and expense account for office staff, entertaining, and travel. Salary: $400,000 per year. Must be willing to relocate to Washington, D.C.

If a want ad were created for the job of president of the United States, it might look something like this. The salary is impressive, the benefits are exceptional, and yet the responsibilities are overwhelming. The job can prove physically and mentally exhausting. Look at pictures of presidents from when they first entered the office and then when they left, four or eight years later—the weight of the office is clearly visible in the way they have aged over a relatively short period of time.

According to *The American Heritage History of the Presidency,* by Marcus Cunliffe, John Adams reportedly said as he was nearing the end of his life, "No man who ever held the office of president would congratulate a friend on obtaining it." And yet, every few years many prominent people declare their intent to run for the presidency.

Who is most likely to win the election? What qualifications and experience are most likely to provide a candidate with the background to become the president of the United States?

The Basics

When you review pictures of the presidents of the United States, two facts quickly become clear. First, they all have been men. Second, until the historic victory of Barack Obama in 2008, they have all been white.

There is no requirement in the Constitution that specifies race or gender of the president, and several women and people of color have sought the presidency throughout the years. The first woman to run for president was Victoria Woodhull, who was a candidate of the Equal Rights Party in 1872. In 1984, the Democratic Party named a woman, Geraldine Ferraro, as its candidate for the vice presidency.

Geraldine Ferraro accepts the nomination.

Elected in 1968, Shirley Chisholm was the first African American woman to serve in Congress. Four years later, she became the first African American woman to make a serious bid for a major-party presidential nomination. She ultimately lost the Democratic nomination to George McGovern.

She and her running mate, presidential candidate Walter Mondale, lost the election to Ronald Reagan. Sarah Palin, a former governor of Alaska, was a vice-presidential candidate when she ran on the Republican ticket with John McCain in 2008.

In 1984, African American activist Jesse Jackson ran for the Democratic Party nomination. He was not the first black candidate for president, however. Shirley Chisholm had run for the Democratic Party nomination in 1972, and other African Americans have run for president on third-party tickets and have sought the nomination of the two major parties in more recent elections.

Hillary Clinton—the wife of former president Bill Clinton—became the first woman to secure the nomination of either of the major political parties when she became the Democratic candidate for president in 2016. Along with the historical presidency of Barack Obama, her victory seems certain to ensure that candidates will continue to become more diverse in the near future.

Working Toward the Presidency

More than two-thirds of all presidents have been college graduates, although a college degree has not always been necessary to win the presidency. Nine presidents never attended college: George Washington, Andrew Jackson, Martin Van Buren, Zachary Taylor, Millard Fillmore, Abraham Lincoln, Andrew Johnson, Grover Cleveland, and Harry Truman. Harvard University has the honor of having the most presidents—seven—as alumni: John Adams, John Quincy Adams, Theodore Roosevelt, Franklin Roosevelt, John Kennedy, George W. Bush (who attended Harvard Business School), and Barack Obama (who attended Harvard Law School). Yale is in second place, with five presidents as alumni: William Taft, Gerald Ford (law school), George H.W. Bush, Bill Clinton (law school), and George W. Bush.

Most (but not all) presidents have had some political experience before their election. Fourteen presidents served first as vice presidents: John Adams, Thomas Jefferson, Martin Van Buren, John Tyler, Millard Fillmore, Andrew Johnson, Chester Arthur, Theodore Roosevelt, Calvin Coolidge, Harry Truman, Lyndon Johnson, Richard Nixon, Gerald Ford, and George H.W. Bush. Others have served as **cabinet officers**, ambassadors, or members of the House of Representatives or Senate.

Nineteen presidents have served as governors of states or **territories**. Six were governor when they became president (Rutherford Hayes, Grover Cleveland, Woodrow Wilson, Franklin Roosevelt, Bill Clinton, and George W. Bush). Only one mayor of a large city—Grover Cleveland, who had been mayor of Buffalo before he was governor of New York—has ever become president.

More than two-thirds of all presidents have had training in the law. Three had no political experience and were elected because of their service as Army generals— Zachary Taylor, Ulysses Grant, and Dwight Eisenhower. Herbert Hoover never ran for any elected office before becoming president, although he had served as secretary of commerce and with several national and international relief agencies during World War I.

Ten presidents served as elementary- or secondary-school teachers—John Adams, Andrew Jackson, Millard Fillmore, Franklin Pierce, James Garfield, Chester Arthur, Grover Cleveland (at a school for the deaf), William McKinley, Warren Harding, and Lyndon Johnson. Six presidents taught at colleges or graduate schools—John Quincy Adams, James Garfield, William Taft, Woodrow Wilson, Bill Clinton, and Barack Obama.

Many presidents, particularly in the early years of the country, owned farms or **plantations**. No doctors or ministers have been elected to the presidency, although William Henry Harrison briefly studied medicine, and both John Adams and James Madison studied religion.

Another common trait of many presidents is personal wealth. Herbert Hoover, Lyndon Johnson, Franklin Roosevelt, and John Kennedy were all millionaires. Thomas Jefferson was the only president to die in debt; James Madison and James Monroe were living close to poverty at the end of their lives.

Most presidents come from small towns or rural areas. Only five were born in large cities, and several (including Andrew Jackson, James Polk, Millard Fillmore, James Buchanan, Abraham Lincoln, and James Garfield) spent their childhoods living in log cabins.

1. How many presidents have served a single term or less?
   a. 5
   b. 13
   c. 18
   d. 22

2. Which president served as chief justice of the Supreme Court after his presidency ended?
   a. Andrew Johnson
   b. John Adams
   c. William Taft
   d. Warren Harding

3. Which president served as director of the Central Intelligence Agency?
   a. George H.W. Bush
   b. John Kennedy
   c. Richard Nixon
   d. Millard Fillmore

4. Who was the only president to marry at the White House?
   a. Bill Clinton
   b. Grover Cleveland
   c. Thomas Jefferson
   d. Lyndon Johnson

5. Which president worked as a movie actor before pursuing a career in politics?
   a. John Kennedy
   b. George W. Bush
   c. Ronald Reagan
   d. Gerald Ford

ANSWERS: 1. d; 2. c; 3. a; 4. b; 5. c

The average age of a president at his inauguration is 54. Ronald Reagan was the oldest, inaugurated to his first term only a few weeks before his seventieth birthday. John Kennedy was the youngest to be elected president, at age 43, but Theodore Roosevelt was the youngest man to *become* president. He was 42 years old when he succeeded William McKinley, who had been assassinated.

President Ronald Reagan with his wife, Nancy, at the Inaugural Ball just after being sworn in as the fortieth U.S. president on January 20, 1981. Reagan was a few weeks shy of his seventieth birthday at his first inauguration, making him the oldest elected president.

Family Life

Family can play an important role in a presidential candidate's success. A candidate's spouse and children often appear during the presidential campaign, and other family members may help raise money, campaign, or even serve on the staff of presidential candidates.

Several presidents had relatives who also rose to the presidency. John Quincy Adams was the son of President John Adams, and President George H.W. Bush's son George W. Bush also was elected president. James Madison and Zachary Taylor were second cousins, and William Henry Harrison was the grandfather of Benjamin Harrison. Fifth cousins Theodore Roosevelt and Franklin Roosevelt both became president.

Most presidents have been married, although not all were married at the time of their election. James Buchanan is the only president who never married. Grover Cleveland, John Tyler, and Woodrow Wilson all married during their presidencies. Tyler and Wilson remarried after the deaths of their first wives.

Most presidents have had children, either their own or stepchildren or adopted children. Tyler holds the honor of having the most children: 15. Most presidential children have been adults or at least young adults by the time their fathers became president. The only child of a president ever born at the White House was a daughter of Grover Cleveland.

Most presidents were born in eastern states, with a slight majority from the north. Virginia has produced the most presidents, with eight (Washington, Jefferson, Madison, Monroe, William Henry Harrison, Tyler, Taylor, and Wilson).

John F. Kennedy's daughter, Caroline (left), and niece Kerry Kennedy play hide and seek underneath the HMS Resolute desk in the Oval Office. Kennedy was often seen with his family by his side throughout his presidency.

President of the United States

The presidency was the creation of a group of delegates, meeting in a sweltering room in Philadelphia. Their vision, their arguments and debates, shaped an office that has produced great leaders, as well as men whose accomplishments are little remembered.

The presidency is much more than simply a reflection of whoever occupies the Oval Office at a particular time in history. Each president brings something unique to the job, but the success or failure of a presidency is shaped by events inside and outside the United States, by events inside and outside the White House. Experienced and skillful cabinet officers and staff members can strengthen a weak presidency; corrupt or divisive advisers can destroy an otherwise successful presidency.

Thomas Jefferson once described the presidency as "a splendid misery," and Adams wrote, when he succeeded Washington as president, that Washington seemed

This 1805 oil painting of Thomas Jefferson is by Gilbert Stuart. Jefferson once called the presidency "a splendid misery." The splendor must outweigh the misery: Every four years, prominent people clamor to run for the highest office in the United States.

to be the only one who looked relaxed and happy at the inauguration: "Me thought I heard him think, 'Ay! I am fairly out and you are fairly in! See which of us will be the happiest!'"

Nonetheless, the presidency remains a potent symbol of what is unique about the American system of government. Every four years, the American people have an opportunity to choose the person they feel is best qualified to lead the country, and to earn a place in history.

Text-Dependent Questions

1. Who was the first African American candidate for president?

2. How many presidents served first as vice presidents?

3. Name one president who married during his presidency.

Research Project

Research a candidate for president from a political party besides the Republicans or Democrats. Write a brief report giving an overview of the political party, its history and agenda, and its current status in the political landscape today, as well as a brief biography of the candidate and how he or she came to the party's nomination. Include information on what the candidate has done since running for office, whether he or she has sought the presidency again, and other significant details.

Series Glossary of Key Terms

Abolitionist: A person committed to abolishing a certain practice, such as slavery or unfair criminal justice practices.

Acquittal: When a person is cleared of a charge of an offense.

Ambassador: A person who acts as the representative of a nation, organization, or other group in discussions or negotiations with others.

Amnesty: To give an official pardon to a person accused of an offense.

Appeal: In legal terms, to apply to a higher court to review, and possibly overturn, the decision of a lower court.

Apportionment: The division of something, such as money, among a group.

Bicameral: Used to describe a legislative body with two chambers.

Bond: A type of financial instrument in which the issuer agrees to repay an investor a certain amount of money with interest over time.

Cabinet: In government, a group of advisers of a head of state.

Canvass: To appeal directly to people in hopes of securing their votes.

Casework: Assistance in matters of government provided by a senator to a constituent, including answering questions, explaining policies, or determining eligibility.

Caucus: A gathering of members of a specific political party or organization to form policy positions, choose leaders, and make other decisions relevant to the organization.

Censure: To formally and publicly express disapproval of a person or action.

Census: An official count of a population, often including other data or information about that population.

Centrist: A politician who favors policies that are neither too liberal nor too conservative.

Chief justice: The highest ranking judge on a court with multiple judges; in the United States, the head of the Supreme Court.

Civil service: The professional public sector of a government (not including the military, judicial branches, or elected officials), staffed by people who are hired for their skills rather than elected or appointed.

Cloture: A means of ending debate on a bill in order to force a vote.

Common law: Laws based on past custom, or what has been judged over time to be lawful or unlawful.

Conference committee: In the U.S. Congress, a temporary committee made up of both House and Senate members, organized to prepare a version of an act that incorporates amendments from both chambers.

Constituent: A person who can vote and is represented by a public official.

Decentralized: Used to describe a system in which power is dispersed among people, states, or other entities, rather than controlled by one administrative body.

Deficit spending: When a government spends money that it has borrowed rather than collected through taxes.

Delegate: A person dispatched to represent others at a conference, legislative session, or other official event.

Demographic: A specific part of a population.

Deposition: Testimony taken down in writing.

Diplomat: An official representative of one country to another.

Duty: A tax or fee placed on imported or exported goods.

Egalitarian: Of or related to the belief that humans are equal, especially with respect to social, political, and economic rights and privileges.

Electoral College: A body of representatives from each state, who formally vote to elect the president and vice president.

Excise tax: A tax on a specific good or activity, often included in the overall price.

Executive branch: The U.S. government entity that enforces laws, with the president at its head.

Extrajudicial: Describing an act that is not legally authorized.

Federal deficit: The amount of money the federal government spends in excess of what it collects in taxes.

Federalist: An advocate of a central national government that unites states and leaves various powers to state governments.

Filibuster: The strategy of legislators talking indefinitely to prevent a vote on a bill.

Franchise: An individual's right to vote.

Gold standard: A monetary system where the value of currency is based on a specific quantity of gold.

Habeas corpus: A legal means by which a person can contest unlawful imprisonment; the term is Latin for "You have the body."

Impeachment: A charge of wrongdoing or misconduct against a public official that may result in termination from office.

Inaugurate: To begin a policy or practice; to formally admit someone into a public office.

Incumbent: A person currently holding a political office.

Indict: To formally charge someone of a crime.

Isolationist: A policy that favors limited or no engagement in international affairs.

Legislature: The assembly of a government or state that is tasked with making laws.

Libertarian: A person who believes completely in the free will and choice of individuals.

Line-item veto: The power of a chief executive to reject certain parts of a bill.

Lobbyist: A person who advocates for particular policies or positions.

Mandate: An instruction to do something in a certain way.

Motion: A formal proposal or request put before a legislative body.

Naturalization: The process of granting a person from one country citizenship of another country.

Originalism: When referring to the U.S. Constitution, a belief that the document should be interpreted along the lines of the Framers' original intent.

Pardon: To release someone of all punishments for a crime.

Parliamentarian: A person who advises a legislative body on matters of procedure.

Partisanship: Strong adherence to a particular cause or group, often at the expense of compromise with others.

Perjury: An act of lying under oath.

Platform: A set of policy goals on which a candidate bases a campaign.

Pocket veto: When a president indirectly vetoes a bill by leaving it unsigned as a legislative session expires.

Political action committee: An organization that raises funds to influence elections, ballot measures, or other legislation.

Polling: In politics, soliciting the opinions of the public to help determine electoral preferences.

Primary: An election within a political party to choose its candidates for a race.

Progressive: In political science, a person who seeks to advance society through implementation of new policies and ideas.

Pro tempore: A Latin phrase meaning "for the time being," used to describe when a person holds a position in the absence of a superior.

Provision: A requirement, restriction, or condition set forth in a legal document.

Quorum: The minimum number of members of a group who need to be present in order to officially conduct business.

Recession: A period of economic decline, with drops in both trade and production of goods.

Reprieve: To grant a delay in sentencing for a crime.

Resolution: A formal proposal adopted by a governing body.

Secession: The formal withdrawal from a state, alliance, or other political body.

Slip law: A document containing the complete text of a new law along with its legislative history, often the law's first published form.

Subpoena: A formal document ordering someone to provide evidence or testimony, most often to a court.

Subsidized: Funded by an outside source.

Suffragist: A person who advocates for others' right to vote.

Supermajority: A vote total that represents significantly more than one-half of the voting assembly, often 60 percent or two-thirds.

Tariff: A tax on imported or exported goods.

Treason: An act of betraying one's country.

Veto: The power to reject a legislative bill and refuse to sign it into law.

Further Reading & Internet Resources

BOOKS

The American Presidency: Origins and Development, 1776–2014. **7th Ed.** By Sidney M. Milkis and Michael C. Nelson. Published in 2015 by CQ Press, Washington, D.C. The most recent edition of this book looks at the relationship of the Constitution to the presidency and focuses on the lives of individual presidents, showing how the office has developed over time.

The American Presidency: A Very Short Introduction. By Charles O. Jones. Published in 2016 by Oxford University Press, New York. This volume in the "Very Short Introductions" series provides a succinct, thorough summary of the presidency, its history, and the electoral process.

Plain Speaking: An Oral Biography of Harry S. Truman. By Merle Miller. Published in 2005 by Black Dog & Leventhal, New York. A new edition of this classic "oral biography" features the thirty-third president telling his story in his own words.

Team of Rivals: The Political Genius of Abraham Lincoln. By Doris Kearns Goodwin. Published in 2006 by Simon & Schuster, New York. Widely acclaimed upon its release in 2006, this study of Lincoln's presidency highlights the ways he brought disparate factions together to preserve the Union.

The Presidents Fact Book: The Achievements, Campaigns, Events, Triumphs, and Legacies of Every President. By Roger Matuz. Revised and updated by Bill Harris and Thomas J. Craughwell. Published in 2016 by Black Dog & Leventhal, New York. This compendium of facts, anecdotes, trivia, election statistics, and behind-the-scenes details has been revised and updated through the presidency of Donald Trump.

WEB SITES

Center for American Women and Politics. http://www.cawp.rutgers.edu. The Center for American Women and Politics, or CAWP, is the nation's leading research institute for information about American women in politics.

Federal Election Commission. http://www.fed.gov. This independent regulatory agency oversees all aspects of campaign finance law in elections. Its Web site features information on campaign finance data, legal resources, and guides for candidates.

Kids Voting USA. http://www.kidsvotingusa.org. A grassroots, nonpartisan organization that offers tools for students and educators to learn more about the voting process.

The White House Historical Association. http://www.whitehousehistory.org. Founded in 1961 by First Lady Jacqueline Kennedy, the White House Historical Association is dedicated to preserving the history and artifacts of the presidential mansion. The association's Web site includes digital archives of architecture, gardens and grounds, fine and decorative arts, and other subjects.

The Miller Center. http://millercenter.org/president. The Miller Center, affiliated with the University of Virginia, specializes in presidential scholarship and political history. Its Web site features detailed accounts of every president, with in-depth essays by noted historians.

Index

Credits

COVER

(clockwise from top left) Joe Sohm/Dreamstime; Steve Cukrov/Shutterstock; Joe Sohm/Dreamstime; Michael Albright/Dreamstime; Daniel Schwen/Wikimedia Commons; Palinchak/Dreamstime

INTERIOR

1, Daniel Schwen/Wikimedia Commons; 11, United States Senate/National Archives; 12, Ramon de Elorriaga/Wikimedia Commons; 14, Everett Historical/Shutterstock; 15, N. Currier/Library of Congress; 18, Wikimedia Commons; 21, ZU_09/iStock; 22, Junius Brutus Stearns/Wikimedia Commons; 23, Everett Historical/Shutterstock; 27 (LE), rdj5150/iStock; 27 (RT), traveler1116/iStock; 28, Pgiam/iStock; 35, Everett Historical/Shutterstock; 37, Everett Historical/Shutterstock; 41, Everett Historical/Shutterstock; 43, Eric Draper, The White House/Wikimedia Commons; 45, Rob Crandall/Shutterstock; 49, Joseph Sohm/Shutterstock; 50, Paul Morse/Newscom; 51, Pete Souza, The White House/Wikimedia Commons; 53, Rob Crandall/Shutterstock; 55, National Archives and Records Administration/Wikimedia Commons; 59, Rena Schild/Shutterstock; 62, US Government/Wikimedia Commons; 66, Joseph Sohm/Shutterstock; 68, UPPA/Newscom; 7, Joseph Sohm/Shutterstock; 71, Everett Collection/Shutterstock; 72, Everett Historical/Shutterstock; 74, Cecil W. Stoughton/Wikimedia Commons; 75, Joseph Sohm/Shutterstock; 76, magnez2/iStock; 79, Steve Cukrov/Shutterstock; 81, Rogers Higgins, Library of Congress/Wikimedia Commons; 84, Mark Reinstein/Shutterstock; 85, Harold Sellers/Wikimedia Commons; 86, Gilbert Stuart/Wikimedia Commons; 93, Joe Soam/Dreamstime; 94, Alancotton/Dreamstime